black pioneers

an untold story

black pioneers
an untold story

WILLIAM
LOREN
KATZ

ATHENEUM BOOKS FOR YOUNG READERS

Atheneum Books by William Loren Katz

Black Indians
The Lincoln Brigade (with Marc Crawford)
Breaking the Chains
Proudly Red and Black (with Paula Franklin)
Black Women of the Old West
Black Legacy: A History of New York's African Americans
Black Pioneers: An Untold Story

Atheneum Books for Young Readers
An imprint of Simon & Schuster Children's Publishing Division
1230 Avenue of the Americas
New York, New York 10020
Text copyright © 1999 by Ethrac Publications, Inc.
Book design by Ann Bobco
The text of this book is set in Simoncini Garamond.
Printed in the United States of America
10 9 8 7 6 5 4 3 2
Library of Congress Cataloging-in-Publication Data
Katz, William Loren.
Black pioneers: an untold story / by William Loren Katz.—1st ed.
p. cm.
Includes bibliographical references and index.
Summary: A bibliographical history of influential African American pioneers and
freedom fighters in the Midwest, including Sara Jane Woodson, Peter Clark, and Dred Scott.
ISBN 0-689-81410-0
1. Afro-American pioneers—Middle West (U.S.)—History—Juvenile literature. 2. Afro-American
abolitionists—Middle West (U.S.)—History—Juvenile literature. 2. Afro-American pioneers—
Middle West (U.S.)—Biography—Juvenile literature. 4. Afro-American abolitionists—Middle
West (U.S.)—Biography—Juvenile literature. 5. Middle West (U.S.)—Race relations—Juvenile
literature. [1. Pioneers. 2. Abolitionists. 3. Middle West (U.S.)—History. 4. Afro-Americans—
Biography.] I. Title. E185.915.K38 1999 977'.00496073—dc21 98-19104

All illustrations are from the author's collection unless otherwise noted.

*To colleague and friend D. John Henrik Clarke
and his pioneer spirit of inquiry*

Acknowledgements

This project has accumulated decades of debts to scholar friends who shared resources, knowledge, and criticism. During her tenure at the National Archives, my dear friend Sara Dunlap Jackson provided helpful shoves, including toward Peter H. Clark, and a microfilm copy of Henry Bibb's great *The Voice of the Fugitive.* Exchanges with the late Dr. John Henrik Clarke, the late Dr. Sidney Kaplan, who provided leads on Michigan and Illinois, the extraordinary Dr. Herbert Aptheker, and indefatigable bibliographer Ernest Kaiser proved both practical and inspirational.

Professors Glenda Riley and Anne Butler, as, respectively, President and Program Chair of the Western History Association, allowed me to present my findings on Black Western women at the 1997 WHA banquet. Also aiding this book were Michigan State University Professor Darlene Clark Hine, whose references to women were masterful; Charles Blockson, underground railroad expert; and Ohio's Beverly Gray and Henry Burke. For years New York University Metro Center director Dr. La Mar Miller granted me access to the great Bobst Library as an (unpaid) "scholar in residence."

Editor Marcia Marshall proffered her usual invaluable advice, but as the one who made decisions, all shortcomings are mine. In a too-long neglected pioneer past, these pages represent a first restorative effort.

William Loren Katz, 1998

CONTENTS

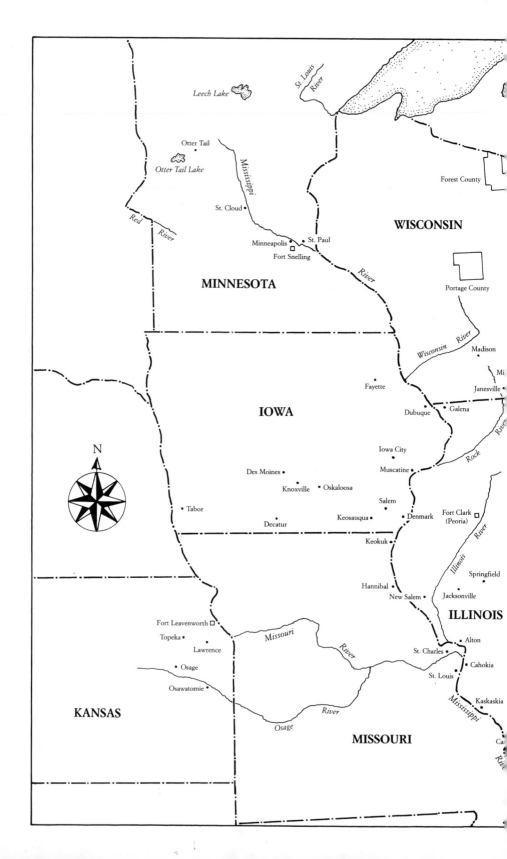

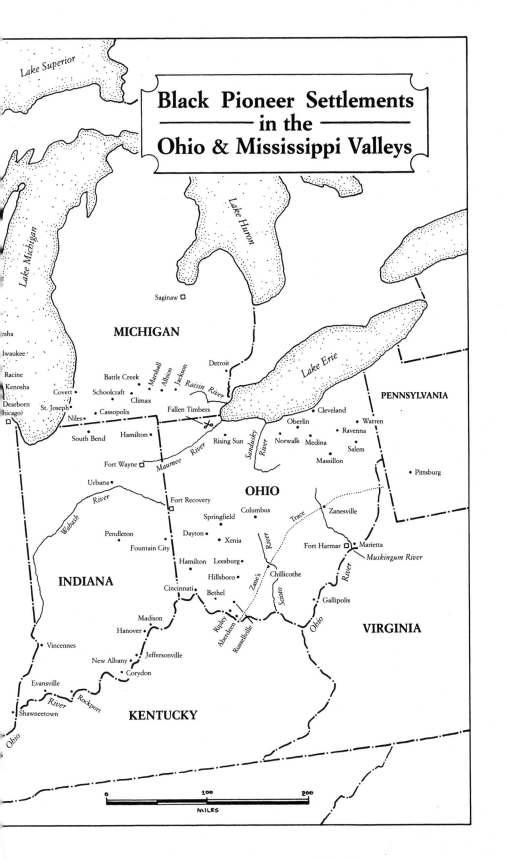

Black Pioneer Settlements
— in the —
Ohio & Mississippi Valleys

Lake Superior

Lake Michigan

Lake Huron

Lake Erie

Saginaw

MICHIGAN

Detroit

Battle Creek Marshall Albion Jackson Raisin River

Covert Schoolcraft Climax

St. Joseph

Niles Cassopolis Fallen Timbers

South Bend Hamilton Rising Sun

Fort Wayne Maumee River

Cleveland

Oberlin Warren

Norwalk Medina Ravenna

Salem

Massillon

PENNSYLVANIA

Pittsburg

Urbana

River

Wabash

Fort Recovery

OHIO

Springfield Columbus

Dayton Xenia

Pendleton

Fountain City

Hamilton Leesburg

Hillsboro

Zanesville

Trace

Zane's River

Scioto

River

Fort Harmar Marietta

Muskingum River

INDIANA

Cincinnati Bethel

Chillicothe

Gallipolis

Madison

Hanover

Vincennes

New Albany Jeffersonville

Corydon

Ripley Aberdeen Russellville

Ohio

VIRGINIA

Evansville

Rockport

River

Shawneetown

Ohio

KENTUCKY

esha

lwaukee

Racine

Kenosha

Dearborn

hicago)

Sandusky River

100 200

MILES

black pioneers
an untold story

Introduction: The Northwest Territory

In 1797 famous trailblazer Daniel Boone entered the Ohio Valley and described its "diversity and beauties of nature."

> Not a breeze shook a tremulous leaf. I had gained the summit of a commanding ridge and, looking round with astonishing delight, beheld the ample plains, the beauteous tracts below. On the other hand I surveyed the famous river Ohio, that rolled in silent dignity, marking the western boundary of Kentucky with inconceivable grandeur. At a vast distance I beheld the mountains lift their venerable brows, and penetrate the clouds. All things were still.[1]

Boone was among the earliest pioneers from abroad to enter the Old Northwest, the valley of the Ohio River. It was a frontier mired in conflict. For many generations this had been the land of the Ottawa, Wyandot, Delaware, Ojibwa, Algonquin, Piankashaw, Potawatomi, Miami, Peoria, Illinois, Kaskaskia, Sauk, Fox, Winnebago, Menominee, and Shawnee. Then in the 1700s France and England, struggling for control of the valley's lucrative fur trade, turned these peaceful Native American villages into battlegrounds.

The British saw rich possibilities growing from the region's furs if they could manage their traders and settlers. Their goal was to license traders, restrict

In 1750 the Ohio Company sent Christopher Gist to explore the Old Northwest. He met with the Delaware, Ottawa, Wyandot, Miami, and Shawnee and found the Ohio River "a beautiful river."

their business activities to designated posts, and then dictate prices. Since profits depended upon a wilderness at peace, Britain intended to purchase Indian lands, fix boundaries, and limit white settlement to reduce conflict.

In 1763, the British victory over the French and their Indian allies gave them control of the Ohio Valley and Canada. With his Proclamation Act of that year King George III aimed to prevent settlement west of the Allegheny Mountains as his first step in dominating trade relations and avoiding Indian conflicts. Aggressive traders and settlers from the east, however, had other plans. When they rushed to displace Indians, their brash actions ended any hope for an orderly transition. British commander Thomas Gage called the intruders "People . . . near as wild as the country they go in, or the People they deal with, & by far more vicious & wicked."

In 1745 British colonial troops marched on the French fort of Louisburg, Nova Scotia, Canada, and captured it.

Ottawa chief Pontiac led a war to drive the British from the Ohio Valley, and in a short time he captured eight major forts in the wilderness. Then British commander Sir Jeffrey Amherst initiated biological or germ warfare. He ordered Colonel Henry Bouquet to "send the smallpox" into Pontiac's villages on blankets and handkerchiefs. He said, "I wish to hear of no prisoners," and in short time the Ottawa were decimated. Pontiac finally settled with his people on the Maumee River, where in 1769 he was assassinated by a Peoria Indian.

By 1774 some fifty thousand eastern settlers had defiantly established homes in the Ohio Valley, men British general Thomas Gage characterized as "too Numerous, too Lawless and Licentious ever to be restrained." In these determined white American frontiersmen, the Indians of the Ohio Territory had a bolder, stronger foe than in the British armies.[2]

The king's proclamation to halt settlement west of the Alleghenies became a key complaint by patriots as they edged toward revolution. The colonists wanted the Indian land west of Pittsburgh and blamed the British for instigating attacks on their settlements by their Native American allies. And there was some truth to that charge.

During the Revolution George Rogers Clark, a surveyor for the Ohio Company, which was interested in the Old Northwest, decided to end British rule there. He convinced Virginia's legislature to claim sovereignty over Kentucky and persuaded Virginia governor Patrick Henry to let him lead a military expedition into the area. In 1778 his band of soldiers swept into the Northwest Territory and captured the British forts at

During the colonial wars in North America, clergymen from France and England blessed and sometimes participated in military engagements.

The Wilderness Road passed through
the Cumberland Gap and led into Kentucky and
the Ohio Valley.

Kaskaskia and Vincennes. The entire Ohio Valley from the Mississippi to Pittsburgh was claimed by his Continental forces.

With the end of the Revolution many veterans of the war saw the fertile Ohio Valley, larger in size than the thirteen original colonies, as their dream of land and farms they could call their own. However, it was still considered Indian territory by the new federal government and claimed by various states. The claims were overlapping. Virginia claimed Kentucky, parts of southern Ohio, Indiana, and Illinois, and land extending to Lake Superior. Massachusetts claimed Maine, parts of western New York, southern Michigan, and Wisconsin. Connecticut claimed land extending from the Pennsylvania border to Ohio, Indiana, and Illinois, and North Carolina claimed Tennessee.

Finally, by 1787, all claims to the Ohio Valley had been surrendered to the federal government so that an orderly westward movement could begin under its management.

Pioneers slowly filled the vast wilderness. More than a quarter of a century later and hundreds of miles west of Pittsburgh, a Quaker pioneer found western Ohio and eastern Indiana with "only a few paths and wagon trails cut through the bushes." Two years before it became the state capital, he wrote of a small village and much empty land: "Indianapolis, the metropolis of the state, was then a new town with few houses. The country between it and Richmond [on the Ohio border sixty miles to the east] was then unsettled."

When this Quaker crossed into Illinois at the Wabash River, he found even more unsettled land. "In the morning we mounted our horses and continued on our journey. This was the sixth day we had travelled without seeing a human being." Reaching the place Springfield now stands, five years after it was settled and fourteen years before it became the state capital, he found a "cluster of cabins" where "all the people were 'squatters' on government land, as it had not then come into the market."[3]

Like the other frontier adventurers, Black women and men trudged into this unspoiled garden with a sense of hope, wonder, and quest. Like the others, their hearts were burdened by two major fears. In an unknown, mysterious land they worried about the dangers of the trail. But even more they feared their efforts to settle there might fail. By foot, mules, horses, and wagons they inched along and were jolted by uncertain roads, sudden storms, and perilous terrain.

Until recently the African American wilderness saga has been lost, shunted aside, or stolen. Scholars wrote of the white men and women who built this country but ignored evidence that people of color had taken part as well. This omission came wrapped in various falsehoods. Some scholars simply ignored evidence of a Black presence. Perhaps it was because scholars chose only to see them as slaves busy chopping cotton in Virginia, the Carolinas, and Georgia. Or perhaps they found it hard to describe African people as brave men and women pathfinders. Some insisted they were not pioneers because only Europeans could survive the wilderness and master nature.

In truth, people of African descent penetrated every frontier. Some lived as members of proud Indian nations. Many survived enslavement to find a free and new life on those lands west of Pennsylvania in the Ohio Valley. John P. Parker wrote of his Ohio experience in the 1830s.

> It has been a matter of great wonder to me, also, to see all the children, rich and poor, going to school. Every few miles I see a school-house, here; I did not know what it meant when I saw these houses, when I first came to Ohio. In Kentucky, if you should feed your horse only when you come to a school-house, he would starve to death.[4]

Parker recalled characters he met who were "ready to drink or fight whatever the occasion might require."[5]

> Don't for a moment ever think that these pioneers were anything except what they were: rough, brutal, sturdy, and strong, with only their fists or a hobnailed boot to enforce their demands. A whole book could be written on the hobnailed boot as a weapon of offense and defense.

But because Parker was also of African descent, his life was markedly different from that of European settlers.

> I had been up to Charleston Bottom [Kentucky] arranging to aid a group of [fugitive] slaves who were ready to start for Canada. It was a dark night. . . .
> Striking a match I read [a tree poster] in large letters: "REWARD $1,000 FOR JOHN PARKER, DEAD OR ALIVE." Not conducive to quiet one's nerves or guarantee one's safety.[6]

Parker's efforts on behalf of slave runaways began soon after pathfinder Daniel Boone left northern Kentucky "still covered by virgin forest, broken here and there by clearings, with many trails and few roads."[7]

The Ohio Valley often had a different meaning for Europeans

and African Americans. Upon reaching Aberdeen, Ohio, runaway Lewis Clarke described his emotions.

> What my feelings were, when I reached the free shore, can better be imagined than described. I trembled all over with deep emotion, and I could feel the hair rise up on my head. I was on what was called a *free* soil, among a people who had no slaves.[8]

His enslaved brother Cyrus reached Ripley, Ohio:

> When we were fairly landed upon the northern bank [of the Ohio River], and had gone a few steps, Cyrus stopped suddenly, on seeing the water gush out at the side of a hill. Said he, "Lewis, give me a tin cup." "What in the world do you want of a tin cup now? We have not time to stop." The cup he would have. Then he went up to the spring, dipped and drank, and dipped and drank; then he would look round, and drink again. "O," said he, "this is the first time I ever had a chance to drink water that ran out of the *free* dirt."[9]

Whatever the Ohio Valley represented for white pioneers, for African Americans who fled bondage it stood for freedom. Free Black women and men who reached the Ohio Valley also arrived as freedom fighters. They had to be. A white legal system created different realities for European and African settlers. In the North, including the Ohio Valley, African Americans encountered territorial and state "Black Laws" that severely restricted their rights and privileges. Adults of African descent could not vote, run for office, serve on a jury, testify in court, take an oath, serve in the militia, or have their children educated in public schools.

In frontier Illinois and Michigan, Black migrants were stopped at state borders and asked to post a bond, usually five hundred dollars, for their good behavior, and show a court certificate proving they were not fugitive slaves. Few carried court certificates and even fewer pioneers of any color carried five hundred dollars. Though officials rarely demanded the bonds, the law discouraged countless families of color from entering these states, and hung over the heads of those who did.

No white marriage faced the tragedy that befell free Blacks Elizabeth Keith of Ohio and Arthur Barkshire of Indiana. In 1854 Barkshire brought Elizabeth Keith, his bride-to-be, from Ohio, and they were married in Rising Sun, Indiana—but Indiana had passed laws limiting Black entry into the state. Barkshire was arrested, charged with bringing his new wife into the state and "harboring" her. The marriage was nullified and he was fined ten dollars.

The couple appealed to the Indiana Supreme Court. It affirmed the original judgment and claimed Arthur was treated "only as any other person who had encouraged the negro woman Elizabeth to remain in the state." The judges warned Elizabeth Keith that she was liable to prosecution under Indiana law. The high court clarified "the policy of the state"—to halt Black migration "and to remove those among us as speedily as possible." It concluded: "A Constitutional policy . . . so clearly conductive to the separation and ultimate good of both races should be rigidly enforced." [10]

When white settlers opened classes for their children, often they turned away African American children at the schoolhouse door. Governments granted funds for public schools and turned down requests by parents of color who paid school taxes. White men marched off for militia duty but not Black men.

White heads of families were able to file for homesteads, but African Americans could be denied the privilege. In 1860 Sylvester Gray, who had homesteaded a 160-acre farm in Wisconsin since 1856, was informed that his claim was revoked because he was "a man of color."

When white men committed crimes against Black women and men, unless a white witness was willing to testify, no one faced trial. On election day white men went to vote and Black men stayed home. In 1839 the Ohio legislature even passed a law denying people of color any "constitutional right to present their petitions to the general assembly for any purpose whatsoever."[11]

Whites could vote, run for office, serve on juries, testify in court, and circulate and submit petitions to the legislature. For these reasons their demands gained the attention of governors, legislators, and judges. But lacking the vote or any other normal access to power, Black efforts to sway the political system bore little chance of success.

As a minority, people of African descent could hold conventions, speak their views, and hope politicians and the media would notice. But their means of redressing grievances were few since they had no base of power. They could ask white settlers to aid their causes, sign their petitions, or contribute money to their schools, churches, or campaigns for equality. They could ask white attorneys and judges for help, and appeal to the courts for relief. But white officials who sat in judgment over their sacred rights had no vested interest in their welfare. Pleas from Blacks to those in power lacked political influence, and Blacks found many who were contemptuous, few who were sympathetic, and fewer still who felt obligated to help.

Instead, pioneer African Americans worked to strengthen their families, communities, and churches and to devise alternative systems of protest and advancement. Churches became ports in every kind of storm. Black ministers promoted ideals of self-sufficiency, manual training, and education. Clergymen and their wives taught adults and children reading, writing, and job skills. Church meetings did more than tend to the spiritual and succor the needy, they served as springboards for community action. Black women and men pooled precious resources to start schools and self-help organizations, and to protect those in crisis.

The Ohio Valley also gave birth to more Underground Railroad stations than any other part of the country. "If Ohio is ever abolitionized it will be by the fugitive slaves from Kentucky; their flight through the State, is the best lecture,—the pattering of their feet, that's the *talk*."[12] So wrote noted antislavery lecturer Reverend Samuel J. May.

African American pioneers of necessity became freedom fighters, and their struggles had much to teach their fellow white citizens about democracy and representative government on the frontier. Their demands were directed toward a government that found no reason to listen. So although their voices spoke bravely, they were rarely successful. But these early frontier men and women posed questions about the American dream and the meaning of citizenship it took a civil war to answer.

This picture was used as an illustration in newspaper ads for runaway slaves.

chapter 1

Black Pathfinders and Native Americans

He discovered "a strong affection between these two races."

Jean Baptiste Pointe Du Sable

The city of Chicago was laid out in 1830, though its first citizen, Jean Baptiste Pointe Du Sable, arrived half a century earlier, in the midst of the American Revolution. However, when he arrived in 1779, the area's British governor, Patrick Sinclair, and his staff hardly welcomed Du Sable to the troubled Ohio Valley. In the middle of the American Revolution the handsome young man bore a French name and accent, and France was an ally of the colonists. He had an interest in the fur trade, which the British were trying to limit for their own profit, and unknown political views.

The original site of Chicago in the late eighteenth century

Du Sable minded his own business, made friends with neighboring Native Americans, and built a small trading post on the Chicago River in what would become the Illinois Territory. Years later Mrs. Juliette Kinzie, whose father-in-law purchased Du Sable's holdings, described how Indians remembered the newcomer: "In giving the early history of Chicago, the Indians say, with great simplicity, 'the first white man who settled here was a negro.'" When trader Du Sable began to negotiate with Native Americans, Mrs. Kinzie also reported, he discovered "a strong affection between these two races."[1]

Du Sable was born in Haiti in 1745, though some accounts place his birth in Canada. There is no doubt that he had an African mother who was enslaved, probably by the French planter who was his father. After his mother died, his father, following a tradition of wealthy French, sent his son off to Paris for a classical education.[2]

Jean Baptiste Pointe Du Sable

22

Black Heritage USA

The founder of the city of Chicago

Du Sable became a seaman on his father's ships and was twenty when he was shipwrecked and badly injured near New Orleans. Needing treatment and rest and fearing Louisiana's planters might enslave him, he stayed with Jesuit missionaries until he recovered.

The young man's wanderings finally brought him to the Chicago River. Shortly before his arrival, colonial commander George Rogers Clark had dislodged the British from forts in the Ohio Valley at Kaskaskia, Cahokia, and Vincennes. More damaging than this military defeat for the British was that France became an ally of the Americans and also declared war against its old rival England. Spain then joined them by also declaring war on England.[3]

As Du Sable settled into his new home, England, the mightiest colonial power on earth, faced a united front of sworn enemies. Colonel Arent de Peyster, British commander of the Ohio Valley, saw his grip on the valley weakening, and viewed the tall French-speaking settler with suspicion.

No evidence suggests that Du Sable took up arms for France, and neither did he volunteer to help the British. However, on July 4, 1779, Colonel de Peyster's report described the trader in these words: "Baptiste Pointe Du Sable, a handsome Negro, well educated and settled at Eschikagou [Chicago], but was much in the interest of the French."

This British judgment spelled trouble for Du Sable. In August British lieutenant Thomas Bennett of the King's Regiment ordered his arrest for "treasonable intercourse with the enemy." Du Sable was held for trial, managed to escape, and was recaptured. Despite both the charges and his escape attempt, he was able to convince Governor Patrick Sinclair that though he had not sworn loyalty to the British Crown, he meant King George III no harm.

After interviewing pioneers who knew Du Sable, Governor Sinclair's staff agreed that the newcomer could be trusted. A new British report found that Du Sable "since his imprisonment, has in every way behaved in a manner becoming to a man of his station, and has many friends who give him a good character." Charges against Du Sable were dropped, and he was released. Then Sinclair asked his former prisoner to serve as manager for a British settlement on the St. Charles River.

For five years, until 1784, Du Sable managed the governor's colony on the St. Charles River, and there were no complaints. To increase his own landholdings, he purchased eight hundred acres in Peoria.

When the Revolutionary War ended, Du Sable hastened to his home at the mouth of the Chicago River in a land now ruled by the United States. For the next sixteen years, he lived by trading furs with Native Americans on the north bank of the river.[4]

Du Sable married Catherine, a Potawatomi woman, probably in ceremonies that followed Potawatomi ritual and custom. By then the Du Sables' log cabin was forty feet by twenty-two feet in size and comfortably furnished with four tables, seven chairs, a French cabinet with four glass doors, a bureau, a couch, a stove, a large feather bed, mirrors, and lanterns. Some twenty-three European paintings he had imported from Paris hung from its wooden walls. This gave Du Sable's trading post an interior unique on any frontier.

In addition to their house, the Du Sable property included two barns, a dairy, a mill, a bakehouse, a workshop, and a poultry house. Although fur trading remained his focus, he also operated a mill and worked as a cooper, making or repairing wooden casks and tubs. The couple owned thirty cattle, two mules, and some hogs, hens, and calves.

The Du Sables gave birth to a daughter, Susanne, and then a son, Jean. Visitors and trappers, white and Native American, were welcomed to their cabin and offered a place to rest and drink liquor. Daniel Boone and Ottawa chief Pontiac dropped in to see their friends and swap stories. As business increased, the Du Sables helped the less fortunate in their village.

As the couple grew older, they adopted the Catholic faith, probably at Du Sable's urging. In October 1788, possibly at his initiative, they journeyed to Cahokia, near East St. Louis, to be formally married by a Catholic priest. Two years later their daughter, Susanne, married a Frenchman, also in a Catholic ceremony. The birth of Susanne's first child made the Du Sables grandparents, and became one of the first recorded births in Illinois.

The Du Sable children, seeking adventure, began to leave home. Their son, Jean, decided he wanted to explore the Missouri River. Susanne and her family moved to a home in St. Charles, Missouri.

As the Du Sable family business expanded, so did their settlement. In 1794 a visitor to the outpost described the six-foot Du Sable as a large man who held some territorial office, was "pretty wealthy, and drank freely."

The Native American neighbors who traded with them respected and liked the Du Sables. Relying on what he saw as his rising popularity, the trader decided to enter an election for chief of the Mackinac nation though he was not a member of the Mackinacs. He lost.

After the election, the Du Sables decided to move. New white settlers were arriving almost monthly, so in 1800, the couple sold everything they had, including their land, to a white trader for $1,200. They left Chicago to move in with their daughter Susanne and her family in St. Charles, Missouri. Illinois was still nine years from becoming a U.S. territory, and eighteen years from becoming a state.

Not long after they moved into their new home, Catherine died. Du Sable began to worry about his own health and his future. He traded in real estate and spoke about wishing to plunge into the wilderness again, but his children insisted he was too old.

Du Sable told his family he never wanted to fall into poverty and would never accept charity. Most of all, the aging trader wanted to be assured he would be buried in a Catholic cemetery.

Jean Baptiste Pointe Du Sable did not get every wish. In 1813, he transferred his house, lot, and other possessions to his granddaughter, Eulalie Baroda. She promised to take care of him and, upon his death, to see that he was buried in a Catholic cemetery. She failed in her promise to care for him, and in 1814 Du Sable had to file for bankruptcy. Then, as he grew older, he had no other choice but to ask for public relief.

Upon his death in 1818, Jean Baptiste Pointe Du Sable's last wish was fulfilled. In a formal Catholic ceremony he was buried in St. Charles, Missouri, in the Borromeo Cemetery.[5]

In 1912 a plaque placed at the corner of Pine and Kinzie Streets, at the heart of Chicago's business district, marked the Du Sable trading post. Among the glass-and-steel buildings it designated the spot where the tall young foreigner had built his cabin and brought his bride.

At Forty-ninth and State Streets in today's Chicago, teachers at the Du Sable High School ask the young men and women sitting in classes to tackle their studies with the tenacity of the Du Sables. The Du Sable Museum on East Fifty-sixth Place offers visitors artifacts and documents that illuminate the contributions made by the founder of the city of Chicago.

John Marrant

John Marrant was born free in New York in 1755. He became the first important Christian clergyman of African descent in

North America, and the first missionary to serve Native Americans in the Ohio Valley.

Marrant was only four when his father died. His mother took him to St. Augustine, Florida, where he "was sent to school and taught to read and spell." His education ended at age eleven when the family moved to Georgia, and he was apprenticed to a Charleston, South Carolina, tradesman.[6]

When John was fourteen, the Reverend George Whitefield, founder with John Wesley of the Methodist movement, arrived to lecture in his town. The teen had planned a prank to disturb Whitefield's oration, but instead the man's eloquence left him "speechless and senseless."

After that, John began to study the Scriptures, and when his family ridiculed him, he left home carrying little more than a Bible and a hymn book. In the woods he starved himself into a religious ecstasy. He also met and befriended an Indian boy, spent weeks hunting with him, and learned his language.

When the two youths stumbled on a Cherokee village, Marrant was seized and tortured. He prayed to God in English, only to find, he claimed, that God asked him to pray in Cherokee. Then he described a miracle. Though he did not know the Cherokee language, he complied with God's will. The chief of the Cherokees and his daughter, in the face of this supernatural occurrence, converted to Christianity, and the Cherokees asked him to stay as their guest.

The Reverend George Whitefield

After nine weeks young Marrant knew the Cherokee language, began to wear their fine garments, and may have considered himself, culturally at least, a Cherokee.

Marrant set out with fifty Cherokees to make conversions among the Creek, Catawar, and Howsaw. But they rejected his efforts, some reminding him that it was Christians who "drove them from the American shores." When he returned to his family in Charleston, Marrant dressed "Indian style."

During the Revolution, Marrant was pressed into service by the British and served for more than six years on a warship. Wounded during a sea battle in 1781, he was discharged and, because he had served the British cause, he left for London.[7]

Marrant heard two callings, one from heaven, and later, one from people of African descent. The first took place when he arrived in London and the countess of Huntington, who had welcomed Black poet Phillis Wheatley to England, took an interest in him. He joined her Methodist church and in 1785 was ordained a minister.

The countess wanted Marrant to become a missionary among Indians in Nova Scotia. After he lectured in London, Bath, and Bristol, he was ready to leave for Canada. Before he sailed, he told his life story to the Reverend William Aldridge, who had it published. The London *Monthly Review* characterized his *Narrative* as high adventure, "enlivened by the *marvelous* and a little touch of the *miraculous.*"

Dedicated to God and Christianity, Marrant's *Narrative* rejoiced in "the Lord's Wonderful Dealings with John Marrant, a Black." He told how miracles were guided by the hand of God and how he had been three times washed overboard from a ship during a storm and three times hurled back by a raging sea. The *Narrative* was reprinted nineteen times.

In 1790 Marrant published his *Journal*, a diary which described his four years in Nova Scotia preaching to native, Black, and white congregations. However, he found white Massachusetts was less receptive when he stood before a Boston parish. Forty men with clubs and swords appeared ready "to end my

A
NARRATIVE
OF THE
LORD's wonderful DEALINGS
WITH
JOHN MARRANT,
A BLACK,
(Now going to Preach the GOSPEL in Nova-Scotia)
Born in NEW-YORK, in NORTH-AMERICA.

Taken down from his own RELATION,
ARRANGED, CORRECTED, and PUBLISHED
By the Rev. Mr. ALDRIDGE.

THE SECOND EDITION.

THY PEOPLE SHALL BE WILLING IN THE DAY
OF THY POWER, Pſa. cx. 3.

DECLARE HIS WONDERS AMONG ALL PEOPLE,
Pſa. xcvi. 3.

LONDON:
Printed by GILBERT and PLUMMER, No. 13, Cree-Church-Lane, 1785;
And ſold at the CHAPEL in JEWRY-STREET.—Price 6d.

evening preaching." Still, he opened a school in the state and began to preach to Black and white congregations.[8]

Marrant's books rarely mentioned racial problems, and he often failed to identify himself as an African American. For many years his primary identification was probably as a devout Methodist and preacher.

In time Marrant became friends with Prince Hall, a highly respected African American civic leader in Boston. Hall asked Marrant to become chaplain of the African Lodge of the Honorable Society of Free and Accepted Masons, and he accepted.

Weeks before George Washington was inaugurated as the first president, Marrant delivered a sermon before Hall's Masons honoring the festival of Saint John the Baptist. Though he lacked much formal education, his words resonated with a poetic eloquence. His sermon celebrated the human family as "the most remarkable workmanship of God" blessed with "the reasonableness of Angels."

He spoke to his fellow Africans of a heritage equal to "the greatest kings on earth." Marrant denounced bigots who used bondage to "dispise their fellow men." He insisted that "surely such monsters never came out of the hand of God."

At thirty-four John Marrant had reached a high point in a life devoted to God and had become the most prolific African American author of the day. His sermons were useful reflections on early American Methodism. After lecturing in Massachusetts for six months, he returned to London in early 1790, and died a year later.[9]

chapter 2

War, Race, and Slavery in the Ohio Valley

*"A multitude of indigent and ignorant people
are but ill qualified to form a constitution and government
for themselves."*

In 1787 the U.S. Constitution was written. That same year the Continental Congress, under a former Revolutionary War officer, Arthur St. Clair, passed the Northwest Ordinance to handle the administration of the new lands west of the mountains. This ordinance has been hailed as a democratic leap into the wilderness since it ensured that Ohio Valley settlers would have a democratic government and also banned slavery.

However, the ordinance was intended as a compact among whites for their benefit. First, it extinguished Indian claims to Ohio and, by opening the valley to white settlers, set the stage for a war with Native Americans that would be completed farther west by the U.S. Army.[1]

Congress began to dole out land grants to Revolutionary War veterans, and families began to cross the Allegheny Mountains into Indian territory. As Conestoga wagons rolled westward, conflicts with Native Americans accelerated, and the cost in lives rose. From 1783 to 1790, 1,500 white settlers died trying to keep Indians from

Packhorses

their lands. Native American losses, never fully tabulated, were even higher. Indians found they were living in a war zone. Every Indian male over age twelve was a potential soldier, and United States policy was aimed at their destruction.[2]

Congress selected St. Clair as the Ohio Territory's first governor and as the first commissioner of Indian affairs. He arrived in the new capital of Marietta in July 1788. Marietta, which had just been settled by a Massachusetts corporation called the Ohio Company, consisted of a dozen log cabins in clearings with a small fortress in the center. Later in the same year, Cincinnati, another fortified log-cabin community, was settled by a New Jersey company. Marietta and Cincinnati faced constant attack by Indians who claimed they had never surrendered their land.

St. Clair's instructions were to "ascertain who are the real head men and warriors of the several tribes . . . and these men you will attach to the United States by every means in your power." This was understood to mean the use of bribes and intoxication, and in January 1789, the governor summoned a council of Indians and forced a treaty on them. By the next year the Northwest Territory had 4,300 white inhabitants and St. Clair prepared to move his government to Cincinnati, part of his effort to push settlement farther west into Indian lands.

As they seized Indian lands by warfare, whites depicted their foes as evil, warlike obstacles to westward expansion. "Traders on the Ohio River attacked by savages" is the caption to this early nineteenth-century drawing.

In April 1789 George Washington was inaugurated as the first president of the United States. The new president and his secretary of war, Henry Knox, pursued policies that presumed a U.S. right to the land. They had no desire to exterminate Indians, and they spoke of negotiations and fair prices. But their series of threats, bribes, and demands told Native Americans they had better leave the lands of their ancestors.

Meanwhile Governor St. Clair soon undermined any possibility of peace. Quick to threaten, late to call conferences, he used minor incidents to blame Indians and end negotiations. He treated them, Native American leaders reported, as "indolent, dirty and inanimate creatures." When the governor finally demanded the entire Ohio Valley, the Indian Western Confederacy responded, "You have extinguished the council fire." When St. Clair spent $3,000 to bribe Shawnee, Seneca, Wyandot, and Delaware leaders to give up their lands, other tribal leaders were enraged, and this made war inevitable.

The U.S. Army was unprepared for war after demobilizing at the end of the Revolution. It had 800 raw recruits, privates were paid $6.67 a month, and Congress refused to increase the military budget. But in June 1790, President Washington ordered elderly General Josiah Harmar into battle, and he managed to assemble 1,453 untrained troops for a campaign in Ohio's Maumee River valley.

His foray slid into disaster as Harmar's guides became lost, his men began to plunder villages, and the general could only restore order by promising an even distribution of the loot. Miami chieftain Little Turtle, or Michikinikwa, lured the army toward today's Fort Wayne, In-

Tecumseh meets General William H. Harrison, who defeated his forces in 1813. To halt the European advance to the Mississippi River, Tecumseh had united thirty-two Indian nations.

diana, where they suffered more than two hundred casualties, and fled home.[3]

In March 1791, Washington asked Governor St. Clair to command an army that would destroy the Ohio Indians. Elderly and suffering from the gout, the governor marshaled 3,000 raw recruits, accompanied by a movable city of 200 women and their children (who served as cooks, nurses, and laundresses) and marched to the eastern bank of the Wabash River.[4]

On November 3, 1791, St. Clair's army had marched a hundred miles north of Cincinnati, where they made camp and went to sleep just south of the site of Harmar's defeat. Few sentries were posted and no other precautions were taken. Just before sunrise a large army of Wyandot, Iroquois, Shawnee, Ojibwa, Miami, Potawatomi, and Delaware overran the camp in a three-hour battle. St. Clair's officers, on horseback and wearing easily identifiable insignias, fell before sharpshooters. His artillery was silenced and captured, and an officer reported that "the whole army ran together like a mob at a fair." Bodies and discarded weapons covered the ground and the wounded were left where they fell.[5]

Weeping officers and men threw their arms away and began a twenty-nine-mile flight for home. The foe "seemed not to fear anything we could do," St. Clair reported, and his men "seemed confounded, incapable of doing anything."[6]

That day the United States suffered its largest single defeat at the hands of Native American forces: 623 soldiers killed, 258 wounded, 24 civilian employees killed and 13 wounded (all but 3 of the women were killed), 69 of 124 officers killed or wounded, and thirty-three thousand dollars in supplies lost, including 400 horses. Of the forces under Little Turtle, only 21 were slain and 40 wounded that day, but more patriots lost their lives or were wounded than in any day of battle during the Revolution.[7]

At a jubilant council, hundreds of Native Americans declared that whites had to leave Ohio, but Washington spent the next two years planning to gain control. He selected General "Mad" Anthony Wayne, a highly experienced officer, as commander of U.S. western forces. Congress voted to double the military budget to one million dollars and increased the U.S. Army to five thousand men. Wayne was ordered to destroy the Western Indian Confederacy and their way of life.[8]

While racial war raged in the Northwest Territory, Mohawk chief Joseph Brant welcomed Black runaways into his Canadian villages.

On August 20, 1794, at Fallen Timbers in northwestern Ohio, Wayne's forces defeated the Indians. His 3,500 troops then fanned out along both sides of the Maumee River for fifty miles, wreaking havoc on Indian villages, crops, and cattle. On November 4, 1795, an Indian delegation asked for peace, and the Ohio Valley was secured for the new nation.[9]

After his humiliating defeat by the Indians, St. Clair returned to govern the Ohio Territory. From 1788 until 1802, he was the region's dominant political figure. He saw the vast Ohio Valley as his personal colony, and, though obligated to consult with the territory's three judges, he ignored their advice and wrote the legal code himself.[10]

St. Clair was a stubborn autocrat, and after assuming power, he organized a militia, banned assemblies, prohibited swearing, and required observance of the Sabbath. He put public order, property rights, and his personal values ahead of the rights of people. He also insisted that frontier citizens were incompetents who could not govern, and expressed his contempt for republican government.

St. Clair, announcing that the franchise to vote was a privilege of the few, limited it to men owning at least two hundred acres, and required officeholders to own five hundred acres. He placed voting booths in distant county courthouses as his way to prevent many farmers from casting their votes.

In the eyes of the governor, Marietta's ethnically and racially mixed population needed discipline. "A multitude of indigent and ignorant people," he insisted, "are but ill qualified to form a constitution and government for themselves."[11]

The year General Wayne vanquished Native American power at Fallen Timbers, Governor St. Clair had an opportunity to enforce the Northwest Ordinance's ban on slavery. As president of the Congress that passed the measure, he was well acquainted with its intent and meaning. An enslaved couple in Ohio (their names are unknown) took their owner, Judge Henry Vanderburgh, to court charging "illegal enslavement" because he had refused to grant them liberty. Citing the ordinance as their freedom charter, the couple brought suit before Judge George Turner. For enslaved people to challenge a master, especially a judge, through the court system required courage, tenacity, and great risk.

The ordinance's Article 6 meant the couple was free "by the Constitution of the Territory," stated Judge Turner, and he ordered them liberated. Defiantly, Vanderburgh had the couple seized and carried off. Turner pointed out that Vanderburgh, sworn to uphold judicial decisions, had committed a "violent outrage against the laws." Then he informed Governor St. Clair that he planned to ask for Vanderburgh's impeachment and removal from office.

At this point Governor St. Clair entered the debate. Though his words lacked any legal or factual basis, he insisted that the ban against slavery did not affect anyone enslaved before the 1787 date. With this wave of his authority, the governor arbitrarily struck down the clear meaning of Article 6. His ruling overturned Turner's decision and did far more. It opened the entire Northwest Territory to human bondage. It invited slaveholders to defy the ordinance by claiming their slaves had been enslaved before 1787.

In nullifying a milestone in the fight for liberty, the governor had turned a law prohibiting slavery into a shelter for slaveholders. The Northwest Ordinance would remain unenforced until people of color and their white allies were able to mount stronger challenges. The battle to restore the ban on slavery continued for many decades.[12]

St. Clair's arbitrary ruling led to other subterfuges. Owners began to arrive in Ohio with people of color whom they now called "indentured servants." They compelled slaves to sign indentures of thirty to ninety-nine years. An *X* marked at the bottom of an indenture document bound the signatory to labor as a servant for life. The territory's number of "indentured" servants began to rise.[13]

Governor St. Clair had one more war to wage against the Northwest Ordinance. The ordinance included clear steps a territory could take to achieve statehood once it had enough citizens. Settlers by the tens of thousands had filled in the eastern portions of the Ohio Territory and demanded the self-rule and statehood promised by the ordinance.

The governor stood utterly opposed to statehood or any other democratic advances for his citizens. But forty-five thousand people called for a convention to vote Ohio into the Union as the first new state carved from the Northwest Territory, and they would not be stopped. In 1800, President Thomas Jefferson's Democratic Republican Party had defeated the Federalists, the party in power under Washington and Adams, leaving Governor St. Clair an isolated man ranting against the wind.[14]

In 1802, thirty-five white men from nine counties, representing forty-five thousand residents, convened in Chillicothe to write Ohio's first constitution. St. Clair, fervently opposed to statehood, accused his foes of "the vilest calumnies and grossest falsehoods." But now his wild charges fell on deaf ears. As a delegate, St. Clair was a desperate man in search of a plan. At one point he urged his supporters to use force to "bring Congress to reason." His ravings against the U.S. Congress and the wishes of his constituents were pathetic and ineffective, and lacked delegate support.[15]

President Jefferson called the governor's plea for violence "evil" and removed him from office. St. Clair left Ohio and sixteen years later died in poverty. By then the Ohio Valley had given birth to two more states, Indiana and Illinois. And Michigan and Wisconsin would soon enter the Union. By the time of St. Clair's death, slavery was no longer protected by law and the state of Ohio boasted more than half a million people including more than four thousand free African Americans.

However, St. Clair's mean-spirited racial views continued to have an impact on the states of the Ohio Valley. The thirty-five whites who met at Chillicothe to write a constitution for their new state faced a dilemma. They overwhelmingly favored strong restrictions on the Black people who lived in the state, and they wanted to prevent the entrance of Black migrants. But they also feared that Congress would reject an Ohio that voted for extreme measures. Ohio's constitution denied its people of color the right to vote but imposed no other restrictions.

The next year, however, the Indiana territorial legislature decided to test the waters further. Indiana legislators passed the first "Black Law" in the Northwest, an act that denied Black people the right to testify against whites in court.[16]

When Congress did nothing, legislators in Ohio had their signal. In 1804 they passed "An Act to Regulate Black and Mulatto Persons," which sought to limit migration by requiring any Black man or woman who entered the state to "furnish a certificate from some court in the United States of his actual freedom." The law imposed a fine of ten to fifty dollars on anyone employing a person who did not show a certificate. This penalty also befell anyone "harboring or hindering the capture of a fugitive slave." Ohio's first Black Law also demanded that Black residents register their names and those of their children with the County Clerk and pay a fee of twelve and a half cents for each name.

Even with this extreme law, African American migration to Ohio continued to increase from one decade to the next. Ohio's African American population, 337 in 1800, soared to 1,899 in 1810 and reached 25,279 in 1850. At one point during the early nineteenth century Ohio had twenty to thirty Black towns.[17]

Ohio legislators, spurred by Indiana's measures and the lack of criticism from the U.S. Congress, passed other restrictive laws. In 1807 they passed a total Black exclusion law which said that no people of color could enter and remain in the state for more than twenty days without posting a five-hundred-dollar bond signed by two white men who would guarantee their good behavior. At a time when few Americans had five hundred dollars to leave on deposit, and few Black people could find two whites in Ohio willing to guarantee their behavior, this meant exclusion. The law was so stringent it could not have been enforced, but it dangled dangerously over the heads of new African American migrants.

Indiana tried three times to pass exclusion bills, and finally compromised with a law that imposed a three-dollar poll tax on all adult Black males. In 1813 the Illinois territorial legislature passed a law that required its justices of the peace to order every free migrant of color to leave the territory within fifteen days. If a person did not depart, the law stipulated that the offender would suffer a whipping of thirty-nine lashes, and this would be repeated every fifteen days until the offender left. These strict laws had as their goal the exclusion of Blacks from each part of the Northwest Territory and set a tone of thinly veiled violence against people of color.

Despite protests and lobbying efforts by people of color and their white allies, these laws became even more stringent in the following decades. Ohio, for example, led the way in extending its Black Laws to deny children of color entrance to public schools or any use of the public school fund.[18]

In each of the five states created out of the Northwest Territory these laws did not end until the Civil War, and then only after pressure from Congress overcame local white reluctance. A single exception came in 1849, when Ohio's legislators repealed its Black Laws. However, this action did not arise from any white political feeling that the laws were unjust or unfair to Black people. Repeal was simply one byproduct of a white multi-party compromise, and had nothing to do with sympathy, justice, or human rights.

It is important to remember that, though the Black Laws were harsh, they remained largely unenforced. The proof lies in the steady growth of the Black population in each state of the Old Northwest. Despite the Black Laws, even those denying entrance to migrants, African American communities were born and expanded in each of the five states that developed out of the Ohio Territory.[19]

chapter 3

Pioneer Farmers of the Ohio Valley

*"The colored people lived well on this food, and were
as sleek and black as the raven. In the spring . . . as soon as
we could erect a cabin, all hands went to work to put
in a crop of corn."*

The first Africans who lived in the Old Northwest Territory
probably were fugitive slaves who had been accepted into Native American villages. In 1669 French explorer René-Robert
Cavelier, sieur de La Salle, discovered Africans living among the
Shawnee. Since French explorers kidnapped Africans from
their homeland, seized Pani Indians in Canada during warfare,
and enslaved other Native Americans in the Ohio Valley, members of these groups often fled to form their own communities
in the wilderness.

Africans also arrived as servants or slaves attached to France's
expeditions into the vast territory that stretched from Pittsburgh westward to the Mississippi River, northward to Canada,
and southward into Louisiana. In 1673 Africans sailed with Father Jacques Marquette and trapper Louis Jolliet down the Wisconsin River to the Mississippi River. In 1703 the new French
Jesuit outpost at Kaskaskia, Illinois, included seventy Africans.
In 1720 Paris banker Phillip Renault purchased Africans to help
build his settlements in the hinterland.

Ohio researcher Henry Burke, whose ancestors were pioneer
settlers, has found evidence that people of African descent lived
among the Delaware nation, who themselves had been driven
into the Ohio Valley from the eastern seaboard. Some of those
who had been enslaved by French and British fur trappers and
hunters also took the opportunity to flee in search of a new life
in the West.[1]

A flatboat on the Ohio River

Migration to Ohio began in earnest after 1786 when representatives of the Ohio Company arrived at the junction of the Ohio and Muskingum Rivers and built a stockade to fortify a town they called Campus Martius. Two years later African Americans were also present when Campus Martius became Marietta, the Ohio Territory's first planned permanent settlement in the new United States.[2]

Other African Americans arrived in the valley after the Revolution carrying claims to land, their reward from the U.S. Congress for their military service during the American Revolution. Black pioneers and war veterans Richard Fisher and Basil Norman settled in Marietta. In 1777 Basil Norman, at seventeen, had been a private in the Maryland Continental Militia. Granted land in Marietta's Third Ward, he moved there with his wife, Fortune. The Normans and their four children stayed in Marietta from 1800 until Basil's death in 1830. In 1996, through the efforts of the Daughters of the American Revolution, a marker with his name was placed in the Mound Cemetery for Revolutionary War Veterans located at Scammel and Fifth Street in Marietta.[3]

On March 6, 1787, at Marietta, James Davis became the first African American born in the newly created Northwest Territory. As a young man, he moved to Dayton, and did his part to assist runaways fleeing from bondage. Davis pursued a successful career as a barber. He was known for his violin virtuosity and contributed to Dayton's cultural growth.

In 1849 Davis organized and served as the first president of the American Sons of Protection, the oldest Black self-help society in Ohio. It was still assisting its members with financial and other problems on January 31, 1891, when J. J. Wheeler wrote about it in the *Cleveland Gazette*.[4]

By the end of the eighteenth century another kind of African American migration was under way. Masters from Virginia and North Carolina were bringing enslaved people across the 1,300-mile Appalachian range to Ohio. Some had been freed before they left the South or soon after they arrived in the Ohio Valley. Some owners did not formally liberate their slaves but held them as servants and allowed them to earn enough money to purchase their freedom. Shawnee Indians from Virginia also sought out new homes in the Ohio Territory and brought their African members.

By 1800 a steady flow of former slaves crossed the Appalachians from Virginia, Kentucky, and North Carolina into Ohio, and many had purchased their own liberty. Once emancipated, free people of color were fearful of living in a slave state where, although free, they were treated as a dangerous force in a society built only for slaveholder and slave. In 1808 the free Black Long community of Africans and Indians left Virginia to settle in western Ohio. Other groups started colonies outside of Cincinnati northward along the Indiana borderline to Dayton, Ohio, and north to the Michigan line.[5]

Samuel Gist, a Virginia master, purchased 1,112 acres near Georgetown and then 1,200 acres in Brown County, Ohio, and in 1818 brought 900 of his former slaves there as settlers.

However, conditions deteriorated for the Gist colony. Many were cheated out of their lots, others fell into poverty because their lands were untillable, and only the few who had the capital and provisions to succeed as farmers survived.[6]

Although free people of color reached the Ohio Valley from Kentucky and more-settled eastern states such as Pennsylvania and Virginia, there were others who escaped from their owners in states of the upper South and arrived with little more than tired, lacerated feet and the clothes on their backs.

Starting in Pittsburgh at the junction of the Allegheny and the Monongahela Rivers, the Ohio River wound its way westward for 981 miles to the Mississippi River at Cairo, Illinois. Some Black pioneers were able to

Farmwork meant long hours and physical labor for young and old.

build flatboats for thirty dollars, launch them westward into the Ohio's waters, and reach such cities as Cincinnati, Louisville, and Evansville. Pioneers used the lumber from these flatboats to create their first homes. They found they had stumbled into one of the world's most productive agricultural regions.

By 1790 a powerful religious force was playing a major role in helping enslaved people reach the Ohio Valley. Quakers from Virginia and Kentucky began to raise funds to purchase slaves and take them westward for a new start. Black communities sprang up alongside Quaker settlements throughout Ohio, but some of the liberated slaves preferred to begin their own communities. As wagon trains of formerly enslaved people rolled into Ohio, the Quakers continued to help. As early as 1816, Quakers in Ohio had formed a Union Humane Society to prevent mistreatment of people of color and help them gain an education.[7]

In 1796 the Ohio Territory boasted two new towns, Dayton and Cleveland. That year Zanes's Trace, the first road to cross Ohio, connected Chillicothe with Zanesville and then went eastward to Wheeling, in what is now West Virginia.

That year one early African American community was started by a devoutly religious white minister and his son. After he was willed fourteen slaves, the Reverend James Finley freed them in Paris, Kentucky. The son recalled how his father's views on God and human nature led to these steps:

> He had been convinced that it was wrong to hold his fellow men in bondage, and thus deprive them of their natural rights; and he was particularly impressed with the belief that there could be no civil regulation authorizing the possession of human beings as goods and chattels, that would justify a minister of the Gospel in living upon the sweat, and blood, and tears of his fellow-beings, as dear to Christ as himself, bought with the same precious blood, and destined to the same eternity of existence. Nor could he bear the idea, for a moment, of involving his children in the evils of slavery.[8]

Once free, two of the party decided to remain in Kentucky, but the minister was determined to help the others reach Chillicothe, Ohio Territory. Finley chose his son James junior, then only sixteen, to lead the party into southern Ohio. The twelve men, women, and children mounted packhorses, which also carried their provisions for the first year. It was not an easy trip, since the western roads were too narrow for wagons. The Allegheny Mountains forced pioneers through "winding paths . . . over-hanging cliffs, and dark ravines," reported an observer. These roads were "crowded with emigrants of every description, but the majority were of the poorest class."

Young Finley wrote of his awesome responsibility:

> My father placed me in charge of the company, though I was but sixteen years old. We carried with us clothes, bed-clothes, provisions, and cooking utensils. We were accompanied with parts of three

families, with a great drove of hogs, cows, and sheep. After we crossed the Ohio river it became excessively cold; and, having no road but a path through the woods, we were not able to travel more than eight or ten miles per day. Some days we were under the necessity of lying by, it was so intensely cold.

After sixteen days of toil and hardship, we reached our place of destination on the bank of the Scioto below Chillicothe. Here we built our winter camps, making them as warm as we could. Our bread was made of pounded hominy and corn meal, and we lived on this together with what we could find in the woods. Fortunately for us, game was plenty, and we caught opossums by the score. The colored people lived well on this food, and were as sleek and black as the raven. In the spring my father and the rest of the family moved out, and, as soon as we could erect a cabin, all hands went to work to put in a crop of corn.[9]

Luckily for the settlers the "soil for richness was not exceeded by any in the world." They found forests of elm, walnut, oak, hickory, and cherry trees, and an abundance of grapes, cherries, and plums. They hunted for turkeys, wild ducks, and other birds. In 1797 their first crop, which included 125 bushels of

Some early settlers sold or bartered wood for other products needed in the wilderness.

corn raised on a single acre, was harvested.

In 1801, as the families feasted on their bounty, an African American in Washington County, Christopher Malbone, stepped forward to become the first and only man of color to vote in Ohio in seventy years. Malbone, the servant of General Israel Putnam, voted for a county delegate to the Chillicothe convention to write Ohio's first constitution.[10]

Though African Americans lived on the free side of the Ohio River, proslavery governments in Kentucky and Virginia made their lives uncertain, precarious, and sometimes perilous. Many of their white neighbors in southwestern Ohio's fifteen counties had come from the slaveholding side of the river and had brought their notions of white supremacy. In 1850 more than a fourth of whites in Ohio were southern-born people who associated Black people with slavery and degradation. They resented domination by slaveholders and feared slaves as labor competitors.

Ohio's first fugitive slave case demonstrated how fragile life in the state could be for people of color. In 1808 Jane, an enslaved

A fugitive is surrounded by a posse and its dogs.

Virginia woman, was convicted of stealing four dollars in goods from a Charlestown merchant and was sentenced to death. Then her sentence was commuted so the state could sell her and keep the money.

But Jane had an independent turn of mind and had made some important white friends. In early November her cell door was left unlocked and she walked out. For the next two days, though in plain sight, she remained unmolested in Charlestown. On the third day she left for Marietta, where she took a domestic job, married a free man, and had a child.[11]

In early 1810 a Virginia mercenary, Jacob Beeson, tried to arrest Jane, but her friends in Marietta made sure that "she was secreted and put out of reach," wrote Beeson in a letter of February 24, 1810. Beeson was a determined man. He persuaded Governor John Tyler of Virginia to ask Ohio's Governor Huntington to extradite Jane. But when some of Marietta's leading white citizens petitioned him for the "justice which is her due," Huntington refused the extradition. Next Beeson convinced Governor Tyler to demand the woman's return under the 1793 federal Fugitive Slave Law. This was the first United States law to provide that slaves who escaped from one state to another had to be returned to their owners when requested. Governor Huntington felt he had no choice but to comply. Beeson reclaimed Jane, brought her back, sold her, and shared in the profits of her sale with the state of Virginia.[12]

In 1835 the forbears of Georgiana Whyte arrived from Virginia. These included Samuel Willis Whyte and his son, who settled near Columbus and purchased two hundred acres. The son, who had been born in 1815, became a medical specialist in chronic diseases. He and Louisa Goode were married and raised a large family, including Georgiana.[13]

In 1920, years after her parents had died, Georgiana wrote of her life with "a loving earnest mother" with a "sweet disposition" who was "often called Saint Louisa." Her father was a "born philosopher," a "keen wit" and a man with "a dash of eccentricity," who became "one of the landmarks of central Ohio in politics and medicine." The family kept its house in good times and bad. Georgiana concluded: "All through Ohio settled

many such high-minded, thoroughgoing Christian Negro families that helped to build up Ohio and left large families, of worthy descendants."[14]

Some of Ohio's early Black farmers were not so fortunate,
however. Abraham Pettijohn, a Presbyterian elder, described
the fate of one settlement: "The land on which they live is so wet
and swampy, as well as very hard to cultivate, that it would be
impossible for the greatest industry and frugality to procure
from it a good living, with the small quantity of land allowed to
each." White neighbors, Pettijohn reported, disturbed the
peaceful community.

> The entire neighborhood in which they settled was
> very greatly opposed to their being located in its
> vicinity—expecting that they would be exceedingly
> troublesome as neighbors—thievish, drunken, quar-
> relsome, strolling vagabonds, and preying upon the
> community. . . . If it is asked how they have suc-
> ceeded, and whether these fearful anticipations re-
> specting them have been realized, I answer, No!
> Quite the reverse.[15]

However, by 1835 African American settlers in this part of
southern Ohio founded a school and a temperance society.

White antislavery figures in Ohio, such as Augustus Wattles,
spent years and his own money to help people of color find land
and an education. In 1834 he began a Cincinnati school for two
hundred Blacks, which lasted for two years. Using his inheritance and raising thousands of dollars, he built schools for rural
Black families in Ohio and Indiana. In one school he taught
leadership development through the innovative technique of
having students rotate as instructors. Wattles also served as an
agent for the American Antislavery Society and helped people
find jobs as skilled mechanics and farmers.[16]

In Ohio, in 1838, Wattles founded a thirty-thousand-acre
colony, which was owned and run by independent Black farmers.
The settlers generated a cooperative spirit with husking bees,

house-raisings, community harvesting, and a united defense against enemies. Families grew mulberries, corn, rye, oats, and hay, and raised cattle; others became barbers or artisans, and all "made a good living."

In 1846, three hundred former slaves of John Randolph of Virginia arrived in western Ohio prepared to farm. The same will that freed them also provided them with forty-five acre-sized tracts. But they were

After weeks of work, members of early Black communities gathered for a dance.

doomed to months of trial and disappointment. Local whites rejected their offer of one thousand dollars for a three-day bond of good behavior, and then escorted them into another county. There they were greeted with hostility: *The Sentinel*, a local paper, stated:

> Every reflecting man must see that the establishment of an extensive colony of blacks in our country must be destructive of the dearest interests and withering to the brightest hopes of an honest and industrious people. . . . No more blacks will be permitted to settle among our people.[17]

Black journalist Martin R. Delany, writing in Frederick Douglass's *North Star* in July 1848, told how these Black pioneers were charged five dollars for a one-dollar tub, adding, "Old horses and plows and other farming utensils, worn out and good for nothing, are frequently sold to them at high prices." That same month, another *North Star* correspondent described a Black Ohio community that found success:

> When my father moved here about ten years ago, it was an almost unbroken forest for several miles around. We had to go about thirty miles for provisions, and then pay an uncommonly high price for them.

In 1839 there were only nine families residing here. The land cleared was not more than forty acres and most of this cleared by "squatters" who came to hunt, etc. We boast now sixty or seventy families of as industrious and intelligent individuals as the surrounding country can afford. There are very few farms less than twenty acres and many twice this amount.

In point of intelligence and mental improvement, the colored people of Mercer County are far in advance of the surrounding whites. We have the best total abstinence society, and the best library of books in northwestern Ohio.

The Randolph excitement has not deterred us from our onward and upward path. The panting fugitive is always a welcome visitor here. God speed the day when life, liberty and the pursuit of happiness shall be extended to all mankind.[18]

**A young man
heads out
on his own.**

OHIO Territory 1799; State 1803

Population growth:

	1810	1820	1830	1840	1850	1860
Blacks	1,899	4,273	9,574	17,345	25,279	36,673
Whites	228,861	576,711	928,329	1,502,122	1,955,050	2,302,808

Bureau of the Census, Negro Population 1790-1915 (DC, G.P.O. 1918)

chapter 4

The Determination
of Sarah Jane Woodson

*"To save thousands of children from want and adults from
public charity."*

In 1793 the inland town Chillicothe, west of Marietta, was built
by sixty liberated Virginia slaves. In ten years, when Chillicothe
became Ohio's first capital, the state had more than three hundred African American residents.

John Stewart was one of the first African Americans to enter
the new state of Ohio. He was was born in 1786 to free Black
and Indian parents in Powhatan County, Virginia. His parents
disappeared, and at age twenty-one, while searching for them in
Marietta, Ohio, he was beaten and robbed. He began to drink,
thought of suicide, and then recovered to take a job that gave
him time to read, pray, and meditate. A later drinking spree was
followed by his religious conversion, which he believed saved
his life.

In 1815, close to death from tuberculosis, Stewart heard a
voice say, "You must declare my counsel faithfully." When he
recovered, he left Marietta to spread Christian gospel among
Ohio's Native Americans. Heading westward, he reached the
Wyandot, near today's Upper Sandusky. For six months he lived
with and preached to the Wyandot. He converted his interpreter, Jonathan Pointer, a man of African descent whom the
Wyandot had adopted. Then he converted several Wyandot
chieftains and their followers. He credited success largely to his
fine voice, which carried his songs of Christian healing and re-
demption.[1]

Stewart's Wyandot congregation initiated the first successful

Methodist mission among Native Americans. He next carried his missionary zeal to northern Ohio, where in 1819 he was licensed as a Methodist minister. After his successes with the Wyandot, the Ohio Annual Conference of the Methodist Episcopal Church established their first official mission to the Indians.

For the next four years, as Stewart preached among the Wyandot, he found time to marry Polly, a woman of African descent. A Methodist bishop who was a friend of his raised cash from Stewart's friends so the couple could purchase a fifty-three-acre farm near Sandusky and build a home.

In 1822 Stewart was visited by Bishop Richard Allen of Philadelphia. After Allen and his followers had been driven from white St. George's Methodist Church in Philadelphia in 1792, they formed their own African Methodist Episcopal Church. After a lifetime within the Methodist hierarchy, Stewart decided to join Allen's church. He concluded that he "could be more useful among his own people than among the whites."

In the fall of 1823 Stewart was confined to bed as his health deteriorated, and that December he died at home. His spoken words live on, however, and for a long time his missionary zeal among the Wyandot also lived on.

In the 1990s a visitor to Upper Sandusky found Stewart's grave beside a small church, buried among his converts. When the Wyandot left Ohio they signed a treaty stipulating that the church Stewart built would remain Methodist.

"That promise was kept," reported the visitor. He also wrote: "The Wyandotte Mission Church stands alone in a block-square park just outside the town center, a tribute to America's first Methodist missionary to the Indians. Just outside the front door of the church, which is surrounded by the historic mission cemetery, stands a memorial to Stewart."[2]

Perhaps no family's achievements better symbolized the potential of African Americans in Ohio than the Woodsons'. Thomas Woodson proudly claimed he could trace his lineage to his mother, Sally Hemmings, a slave, and that his father was her master, Thomas Jefferson. As of 1998, DNA evidence strongly suggests that Jefferson was the father of Hemmings's children.

Through hard work, Thomas Woodson was able to earn enough money to purchase his wife and family from Virginia planter Jacob Price for about nine hundred dollars each. Woodson had previously visited Ohio, possibly in a cattle drive, and in 1820 he packed his family into a Conestoga wagon and, along with the Leaches, the only other free Black family in Greenbriar, Virginia, made the journey into Ohio.[3]

The Woodsons arrived penniless in Chillicothe but were welcomed by white abolitionists of the Chillicothe Presbytery, a network of committed antislavery ministers who influenced religious training in Ohio.[4]

Soon after settling in Chillicothe, the Woodsons joined the Methodist church, only to be assigned to its northern gallery. They sat apart from whites and had to take communion last. Protesting this, Thomas Woodson pointed out that they "contributed their share in supporting ministers and defraying the contingent expenses of the church."

In 1821 Chillicothe's Black families responded to this discrimination by organizing their own Quinn Chapel African Methodist Episcopal Church, the first AME branch west of the Allegheny Mountains.[5]

Sarah Woodson was born in November 1825, one of the youngest of eleven children. Her education proceeded rapidly. By three she could sing from the Methodist hymnal, and at five she could recite Bible passages. As she grew up in the 1830s and 1840s, three of her brothers, Lewis, Thomas, and John P., became well-educated and licensed ministers in African American churches.

The AME church was more than a house of worship for African American families on the frontier. Members, particularly women, embraced its teachings

In Ohio, where this congregation met, and throughout the North and West, Black people found hope and protection in their churches.

as community standards and pledged themselves to hard work, education, and temperance. Women dressed plainly, rejecting exotic jewelry and garish or fancy clothing, and devoted their free time to religious contemplation and study, and community and self-improvement.

Education was a cardinal Woodson goal. When she was about two Sarah began her education at the African Education and Benefit Society, where she was taught by her brother Lewis. By then children of color had been excluded from Ohio's public schools, and Black communities had begun to prepare their own teachers and create their own classrooms, often in connection with their churches.[6]

In 1829 the Woodsons and other African American families responded to local bigotry by moving forty miles away from Chillicothe to Berlin Crossroads, Jackson County, to begin their own farming community. The community pitched in to build a church, a day school, and a Sunday school. By 1840, twenty-three families of color lived in Berlin Crossroads, and the Woodsons were prominent and respected community figures. Thomas owned four hundred acres and several thousand dollars in other real estate, and ten years later his wealth had reached fifteen thousand dollars. A Woodson cemetery was built and still bears a family marker.[7]

Sarah grew to womanhood among self-educated, independent, landowning men and women who tended their own crops and came home each night to study around a fire. In 1842 a neighboring white farmer told a local paper that the African Americans he saw cared more about their children's education than whites he knew.

Residents of Berlin Crossroads who visited Chillicothe reported they were treated with greater respect than the town's own African American residents.

The AME Church and its Bible remained at the heart of the Woodson philosophy. As a child in the 1830s Sarah Woodson was thrilled to watch her mother and other dynamic women feed dozens of people at giant religious revival festivals. By age fourteen, when she joined her mother's church, the Bible provided Sarah with tales of women like Lydia, who prayed to be

God's messenger. She was further delighted when Jarena Lee, a woman of color and a preacher, gave a sermon at her church. Religion unlocked doors to a new world of activism for Sarah Woodson.[8]

Sarah was twenty-three in 1848 when the AME General Conference debated licensing women ministers to spread the gospel. That same year white women at Seneca Falls, New York, launched a movement to secure their citizenship rights, including the right to vote.

In 1830, in Philadelphia, Sarah's oldest brother, Lewis, took part with other members of the country's Black intellectual elite in the historic first National Black Convention. The next year he moved to Pittsburgh, where he began a career in education and reform. He became a Methodist minister, began a school for African Americans, and was admitted to membership in the city's American Moral Reform Society. But his ultimate goal was to create separate societies for his people led by the AME Church and directed by its clergymen.

Lewis planned churches and schools to encourage his people to "free themselves from their traditional dependence on whites." He thought that white ministers were too prejudiced to serve people of color, and said African American churches had to be "identified with ourselves." Sarah believed that her church did "more to convince the world that colored men possessed a high degree of the power of self-government, and that their hearts swelled with the same love of liberty which animated the hearts of the most noble of earth's sons."[9]

In 1850 Sarah Woodson left Berlin Crossroads to study at the Albany Manual Labor Academy. As an integrated school in southern Ohio, it offered, according to an AME Church booklet, "a social and civil atmosphere in which the colored man can breathe equality with others." Two years later, Sarah and her older sister Hannah enrolled in Oberlin College, recommended by the AME as one that accepted African American pupils.

At Oberlin the two young women found the moral reform atmosphere they had enjoyed in Berlin Crossroads. The pupils at the college were fervently antislavery, tried to reject racial

Sarah
Jane
Woodson
about the
time she
attended
Oberlin

stereotypes, and shared a devotion to education and religion. The Woodson sisters easily adjusted to their classmates of both races and attended the town's Congregational church.[10]

Oberlin College was unique. In 1835, two years after it was founded, it announced that "the education of people of color is a matter of great interest." Its first Black pupil was James Bradley, a former slave, and its enrollment remained at about 95 percent white and 5 percent Black. For thirty years, until 1865, Oberlin trained 140 Black women from the North and South, many referred by abolitionists.

After growing up in African American communities, for the first time the Woodson sisters at Oberlin found themselves a distinct minority. After a year or two in the college preparatory program, Hannah left, but Sarah stayed on to complete the four-year course. She used money provided by her father,

Osborne Perry Anderson attended Oberlin College and joined John Brown's 1859 raid on Harpers Ferry. He survived, wrote a book about his antislavery adventures, and fought in the Union army during the Civil War. [Library of Congress]

borrowed from her inheritance, and during vacations taught in Black elementary schools to defray additional expenses.[11]

Oberlin officials did not completely conquer bigotry. In 1860, Emma Brown, an African American student, wrote, "There is considerable prejudice here, which I did not at first perceive." However, African American students graduated from Oberlin, some with high honors, and many enjoyed distinguished careers in education. For example, in 1871 Mary Jane Patterson, who graduated in 1862, became the first Black woman principal of a Washington, D.C., high school.[12]

Wilberforce College, near Xenia, Ohio, was an early interracial school founded in 1856 by the Methodist Episcopal Church.

In 1856, when Woodson graduated, few men of any race and even fewer women, had college degrees. But in that year her brother Lewis was named one of four Black trustees of what became Wilberforce College in Xenia, Ohio. He proclaimed that his high purpose was to adorn his people's "minds with that jewel that will elevate, ennoble, and rescue the bodies of our long injured race from the shackles of bondage, and their minds from the trammels of ignorance and vice."

In the decade after her graduation Sarah Jane Woodson devoted herself to teaching in Ohio's AME schools at Chillicothe, Gallipolis, Zanesville, Hillsboro, and Hamilton. At one point she also returned to teach at Berlin Crossroads and live with her parents.[13]

Then she was hired to teach at Wilberforce College. Her academic career was not without its dramatic moments. In 1862, while she was on the Wilberforce faculty, someone set fire to a building and a white woman instructor suffered a nervous breakdown. When Woodson was offered her open post, she quickly accepted the promotion.[14]

In 1866 Wilberforce College promoted her to a "Professorship," which it called "Preceptress of English and Latin and Lady Principal and Matron." This made her the first African American woman to be granted full college faculty status. Oberlin College would not hire a Black woman professor for another century.

With the Civil War over Woodson decided to focus on those former slaves who had begun to seek education. The Ku Klux Klan night riders often targeted African American schools, teachers, and pupils, but Woodson was undeterred. In 1868 she took a teaching job at Hillsboro, a North Carolina girls school, and soon faced what she called "danger and difficulty." An administrative report found her classes "thoroughly disciplined, and the children making rapid progress in their studies and all that pertains to a well-ordered school life."

Then, in September, Sarah Woodson's life changed. At forty-three she and the Reverend Jordan Winston Early, fifty-three and a widower with several young children, were married. Early had been born a slave in 1814, become free, and at age twelve became a minister in St. Louis, though he would not learn to read until he was eighteen. In 1836 Early began to organize AME churches in St. Louis and New Orleans. The Church characterized this era as "perilous times" when only "men and women of brave hearts, true courage and daring" could succeed.[15]

Mrs. Early left North Carolina for Tennessee, where for the next eighteen years she taught in cities where her husband's churches were located. She also worked with her husband's congregations, "assisting in all of his most arduous duties, and sharing most cheerfully with him all his hardships, deprivations, and toils." She supervised Sunday schools, led prayer meetings, visited the ill, aided the poor and needy, and raised funds for the church. She described herself as one of those committed women "ready, with their time, their talent, their influence, and their money, to dedicate all to the building of the church. No class of persons did more to solicit and bring in the people than they."

In 1888, when Jordan Early retired, Mrs. Early had been an educator for thirty-two years, had instructed six thousand children, and had served as a principal in four cities. She continued to teach, joined the temperance movement, and from 1888 to 1892 directed the Colored Division of the Women's Christian Temperance Union. She lectured for the Prohibition Party in Tennessee and by 1889 she had carried its message to seventy-five churches, twelve colleges, and five prisons. She was proud of her 130 lectures, her talks with three hundred ministers and educators, and her hundreds of essays on temperance.[16]

At the 1893 world's fair in Chicago Mrs. Early was named "Representative Woman of the Year," and that year her life story was featured in two books. Though pleased, she noted that women of color had "waited for moral and intellectual recognition from the world" for a long time.[17]

Mrs. Early urged women to take stands on public issues, and "a more exalted position, . . . assuming the more responsible duties of life with their favored brothers." She praised the efforts of Black women and men to build self-help societies "to save thousands of children from want and adults from public charity."[18]

In 1895, years after Mrs. Early and others had sown the seeds, the National Association of Colored Women was formed. In 1907, at age eighty-three and four years after her husband's death, Sarah Woodson Early died. Black women, she once said, could be "as strong as giants."

One biographer has called Sarah Jane Woodson Early "a black activist" who believed in "black separatism and self help," and "a black feminist as well as a black nationalist." In her own quietly assertive pioneering way, she showed that African American women could change the world.[19]

chapter 5

Peter H. Clark's Cincinnati

"Against these national and state wrongs it is our duty to protest."

Cincinnati, on the Ohio River across from Kentucky, provided trade links to Pennsylvania and other eastern markets in the Northeast. But because the Ohio also flowed southwest into the Mississippi River, its trade was controlled by slaveholders. They shaped the city's economy, influenced its political outlook, and posed a threat not only to runaways but to free people of color. Slaveholders and African Americans warily eyed each other on the dusty streets of Cincinnati. By appealing to the city's poor whites for racial solidarity, slaveholders turned Cincinnati into an early flash point in the struggle over human rights.[1]

By 1820 Cincinnati's 2,258 African Americans formed a tenth of the total population, and most were congregated in the wooden shacks that formed "Little Africa"s in two distinct parts of the frontier town. This Black presence provoked mounting fear from the city's wealthy whites, largely men who did business with and were sympathetic to southern slaveholders. In 1826, 120 white businessmen formed a Colonization Society that aimed to lure African American citizens with a free ticket to Africa. But Blacks showed little interest.[2]

In 1829 Cincinnati's poor whites,

Early picture of Fourth Street in Cincinnati

fearful of competition from free Blacks for low-paying jobs, talked of evicting Cincinnati's Black citizens. That June, city officials issued an ultimatum telling African American residents to leave by September. In August, to speed matters, two hundred to three hundred white rioters charged into African American neighborhoods. Armed people responded, and a white leader was slain. At this point many African American citizens, including the most industrious, and those with the most to lose, left to settle in what would become Wilberforce, Canada.[3]

In Cincinnati in the 1830s, young Harriet Beecher Stowe helped escaping slaves and later wrote the novel *Uncle Tom's Cabin.*

More racial sparks flew in 1836 when James G. Birney, a former Alabama planter who had liberated his slaves, settled in Cincinnati and began to publish an antislavery paper, the *Philanthropist.* A mob led by some of the town's wealthiest citizens burst into Birney's offices, dismantled his press, and carted it off. Birney rebuilt his business only to have another mob arrive, drag his press down Main Street, and throw it into the Ohio River.

The threat of violence continued to hang over the port city. In September 1841, hundreds of whites from Kentucky marched into Cincinnati carrying clubs, stones, and guns and dragging a cannon. What followed was a night of mayhem against African Americans. "Our city has been in complete anarchy, controlled mostly by a lawless and violent mob for twenty-four hours, trampling all law and authority under foot," announced an editor the next day.[4]

Even so, by the end of the decade some African Americans were able to gain a foothold on the economic ladder. In 1847

A scene from *Uncle Tom's Cabin.* Eliza comes to tell Uncle Tom she is fleeing to save her child. The novel is based on author Harriet Beecher Stowe's Ohio experiences. [Library of Congress]

Robert Gordon purchased his freedom in Virginia, ran a coal business there, then sold it for fifteen thousand dollars and went to Cincinnati. There he started his own coal business, hired bookkeepers, and built an empire of wagons, docks, and barges. When white competitors conspired to ruin his business, he managed to defeat them and became even wealthier. He retired in 1865, and died in 1884 a rich man.[5]

Other people of color found economic success in Cincinnati, too. Samuel T. Wilcox, born poor, invested in real estate and began a grocery store that became the city's "most extensive business house of its kind." Henry Boyd's bedstead factory employed two dozen workers and filled "orders from all parts of the West and South." The Bowers brothers ran a fancy tailoring establishment.[6]

Before the Civil War Cincinnati's Black community had created five schools, five churches, eleven self-help societies, and an orphanage. Its women of color took a vital part in building these cultural centers.[7]

In 1848 housewives organized a hot reception for slave catchers who arrived to recapture eight to ten slaves who had crossed the Ohio River in early August. Frederick Douglass's *North Star* reported the clash:

One Saturday, hot and heavy, came the bloodhounds in quest of their prey—bowie knives in their pockets and revolvers in their hats.

The women began to gather about the adjoining houses until the Amazons were about equal to the [slave catchers]—the former with shovels, tongs, washboards and rolling pins; the latter with revolvers, sword-canes and bowie knives. Finally the besiegers decamped, leaving the Amazons in possession of the field, amid the jeers and loud huzzahs of the crowd.[8]

In 1847, after twenty years of aiding escapees in Indiana, where he was known as "the President of the Underground Railroad," Quaker Levi Coffin moved to Cincinnati. Levi and Sarah Coffin learned that white residents of the city were fearful of aiding fugitives, and Black residents lacked the funds. The couple inspired trustworthy volunteers of both races. Black men acted as wagon drivers, assisted by young white men. A white women's society assembled weekly at the Coffin home to sew clothing for the underclad escapees.[9]

Perhaps the world's most electrifying incident of resistance began to unfold in Cincinnati with the escape of seventeen armed runaways in January 1856 from Boone County, Kentucky. Among them was pregnant Margaret Garner, twenty-two, "about five feet high, showing one fourth or one third white blood," "eyes bright and intelligent." Mrs. Garner bore a scar from her forehead to her cheekbone because, she reported, "a white man struck me."[10]

Garner, her husband, Simon, and their four children raced along icy roads in sleds and then walked across the frozen Ohio River to Cincinnati. When the family was surrounded by slave hunters and U.S. marshals, Mrs. Garner, saying she would rather they died than return to bondage, killed one of her daughters.

In a Cincinnati court Mrs. Garner sat with her nine-month-old daughter, her two sons, ages four and six, and an "expression of settled despair." Despite protests by whites and Blacks, President Franklin Pierce ordered the Garners returned to bondage. But, in Kentucky, Garner drowned another child. The

Garner tragedy convinced a young white Ohio attorney of the day, Rutherford B. Hayes, to declare, "From this day forward, I will not only be a black Republican, but I will be a damned Abolitionist." The incident also served as an inspiration for Toni Morrison in writing her novel *Beloved.*[11]

Efforts on behalf of escapees continued. In 1858 William M. Connelly, a white man, was tried for harboring a fugitive in Cincinnati. When he was sentenced to twenty days' imprisonment and fined ten dollars, his sympathizers staged demonstrations. The city's African American women brought strawberries, pastries, and other tasty food, and comfortable furniture to his cell. Prominent Methodists and Unitarians convening in the city visited him. On the rainy evening he was released from jail, he was greeted by a parade that included a local German American social society, a uniformed band, and Republican politicians.[12]

Margaret Garner has slain one of her children rather than see them returned to slavery. Engraving from a painting by Thomas Noble.

Peter H. Clark

Peter H. Clark was born in 1829 in Cincinnati when rioting had driven out many of the Black community's leading figures.

His family, however, decided to remain. This son of a local barber grew up to become Cincinnati's leading African American intellectual. He graduated from the best schools open to a young man of color in the city, and in 1844, in the first year it opened, he entered Gilmore High School, the first secondary school for African Americans anywhere in the former Ohio Territory. Two years later, and still a teenage student at Gilmore, he was appointed a teacher there and found his calling.

In 1849, the young man became an instructor at the first public school to be opened specifically to serve African Americans, but no public funds were voted for it. During these early years, young Clark assisted runaways who reached the city to escape posses bent on their return.[13]

Clark was a short, wiry, intense man with a personality that noted historian George Washington Williams characterized as "sarcastic, industrious, earnest, nervous, and even practical at times." He apprenticed for a year to a printer to learn the trade, and, in 1852, as his people faced the new, harsh Fugitive Slave Law and rising white bigotry in the North, Clark began to urge a Black emigration to Liberia. The next year he was chosen the national secretary of the Black Convention that met in Rochester, New York, and later that year he drafted the constitution for the National Equal Rights League and attended another Black convention in Syracuse, New York.[14]

Educator
and activist
Peter H. Clark

In 1855 Clark briefly published a crusading Ohio weekly, *The Herald of Freedom*, the first African American newspaper in the Middle West. He also contributed articles to Frederick Douglass's *North Star.* Through his presence at conventions and his published work, Clark was recognized as a national leader among his people. He became increasingly active in political life, too, speaking for the Republican Party from its founding in 1856.[15]

In 1857 Clark's dream of a career in education was finally fulfilled when he was appointed principal of the Western District Colored School in Cincinnati. In response to the growing Black population in the city, he urged the establishment of additional Black schools.

Peter Clark had always been intensely aware of Cincinnati's alliance with slaveholders. In 1860 he publicly noted that William Yancy, a Confederate "fire-eater," was allowed to make a speech that called for dissolution of the Union and received a polite reception. A short time later, however, Wendell Phillips, the noted abolitionist orator, appeared, only to be "driven from the same platform by mob violence."[16]

During the Civil War Clark characterized what African American citizens faced in their hometown:

> The city of Cincinnati always has been, and still is, proslavery. Nowhere has the prejudice against colored people been more cruelly manifested than here. Further north or further south the feeling is not so intense; but here it almost denied him the right of existence.[17]

Nevertheless, Black men born in the city were ready to defend it during the Civil War, even before their emancipation. In 1862 Cincinnati was threatened by John Morgan's Confederate raiders and Black men formed a brigade to fight for their city. Bigoted white citizens influenced official policy, however, to deny Blacks arms and employ them not as soldiers but laborers. Nevertheless, to do their part, the men proudly built miles of roads, dug rifle pits, and cleared acres of land. The veterans then chose Clark as their historian and he wrote *The Black Brigade of Cincinnati*, telling of their contribution to the defense of the city despite many obstacles.

When the Civil War led to emancipation, Black Cincinnati citizens were determined to secure their citizenship rights. In 1864, late in the war, the *Colored Citizen*, a Cincinnati newspaper, served as the voice of African American attorney and

activist John Mercer Langston and his newly formed Equal
Rights League. In a fiery editorial, the paper welcomed emancipation.

> American society is in a state of revolution. The
> armed slave confronts his master on the field of bat-
> tle. They whom the highest judicial authority in the
> country pronounced aliens in the land of their birth,
> are solemnly declared citizens, and invited to share
> in the perils of those who are striving to maintain the
> Union, which happily has become, to us and our
> children, the bulwark of liberty. . . . In nearly all of
> the States we are denied the elective franchise. . . .
> Against these national and state wrongs it is our duty
> to protest.[18]

In January 1865, the Ohio Equal Rights League met in Xenia
to demand "the repeal of all laws and parts of laws, State and
National, that make distinctions on account of color." By then
Cincinnati and Ohio were in the process of ending all Black
Laws denying the privileges of citizenship to their African
American residents.[19]

In 1866 Clark was appointed principal of Gaines High
School, a job to which he would devote the next thirty years of
his life. He trained more than a generation of teachers at a time
when millions of former slaves finally had their opportunity to
get an education for themselves and their children.

Clark's reputation as a progressive educator led to his being
appointed the first school superintendent of color in the state
and a trustee of Wilberforce University.

In July 1877, during the first week of the country's tumultuous
earliest nationwide rail strike, he addressed striking workers in
Cincinnati. Clark's oratorical skills had grown, and so had his rad-
icalism, for he spoke for the poor regardless of color, condemned
greedy corporations, and advocated a system of state socialism.

That year he had also joined the Workingmen's Party of the
United States, spoke on their behalf in Ohio and Kentucky, and
ran on their ticket for Ohio state superintendent of schools and
lost. He advocated consumer cooperatives, denounced extreme

During the first nationwide railroad strike in 1877, Peter H. Clark sided with the workers and urged radical social reforms.

poverty and wealth as dangerous to democracy, and demanded that capitalism surrender "some of its assumed selfish rights and give labor its share."

In 1877 Clark became the first known Black advocate for a socialist state. To the working people of Cincinnati he said that "the government must control capital with a strong hand," and he advocated federal control of all rail lines. He predicted that in twenty years this would come to pass:

> [T]here will not be a railroad in the land belonging to a private corporation; all will be owned by the government and worked in the interests of the peoples. Machinery and land will, in time, take the same course, and cooperation instead of competition will be the law of society. The miserable condition into which society has fallen has but one remedy, and that is to be found in Socialism.

Clark ended his speech to the strikers by saying, "The future is ours." In the following weeks, scores of men of both races died when federal troops, ordered to end the strike, opened fire on them in several cities. Clark lived until 1925 and saw greater federal regulation of railroads. But he never saw his dream of a United States without extremes of wealth and poverty, managed in the interest of working men and women of all races.[20]

chapter 6

A Railroad's "Fierce Passions"

"How they crossed the numerous creeks that lay waiting for them like a trap was unbelievable to me. As a matter of fact, they became backwoodsmen, following the north star, or even mountains, to reach their destination, the Ohio river."

Many courageous men and women of color served as conductors for the Underground Railroad in the years before the Civil War, and this chapter will focus on three African Americans who operated in the Ohio Valley: William M. Mitchell, John P. Parker, and Henry Bibb.

William M. Mitchell

Many books tell the story of the Underground Railroad, but only one was published by its author when it was still a federal crime to aid fugitives. William M. Mitchell's *The Underground Railroad* (London, 1860) was a daring book by a daring conductor. Although he was

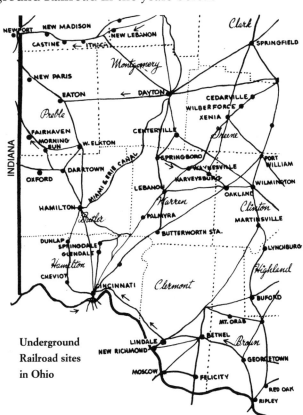

Underground Railroad sites in Ohio

born free in North Carolina, Mitchell's parents died early in his life, and he was apprenticed for twelve years to a planter. In the last five years of his indenture, he was manager of what he termed—but never described—as the plantation's "disgusting details."

Mitchell, who escaped to Ohio, became a devout Christian, then an ordained minister, and finally a man who tried to help fugitives. He was drawn into the work by the tragedy of a Maryland slave man who escaped in 1843, married, had three children, and joined a Methodist congregation in Ross County, Ohio. The family was betrayed by its white minister, who was paid one hundred dollars by a bounty hunter to turn him in. When three slave catchers seized the man and sped him out of town, Mitchell saw the Black community rally "200 strong, in little or no time."

The rescuers caught up to the three mounted men, who dragged their prisoner at the end of a rope attached to a horse. As the rescuers shouted and threatened, the Marylanders decided to cut the rope and flee. The African American commu-

Abolitionists helped slaves escape. But their propaganda rarely showed escapees fighting back. This drawing shows armed whites and African Americans arrayed against slave hunters. [Library of Congress]

nity shouted for joy and bore their friend on their shoulders. In this way, Mitchell found a new calling.[1]

> I was initiated into this underground business in the county of Ross, in the State of Ohio, in 1843, and continued in the office, faithfully discharging the duties, until 1855. Never for one moment have I regretted being thus engaged, though I experienced many very unpleasant things during that period. . . . Many have been the times I have suffered in the cold, and beating rains pouring in torrents from the watery clouds. In the midst of the impetuosity of the whirlwinds and wild tornadoes, leading on my company. Not to the field of sanguinary war and carnage, but to the glorious land of impartial freedom, where the bloody lash is not buried in the quivering flesh of the vassal.
>
> The distance which they are led in a night varies. I have taken them 20 miles in a night, but that is not the usual distance, 6 to 12 miles is more commonly the length of each journey.

He also wrote of the religious origins of his work:

> God has commanded us to assist the poor and needy; the helpless, the outcast, and the downtrodden. . . . He made a provision for the Fugitive Slave. He commanded first of all, that Israel should not turn him back or deliver him to his heathen master whom he had fled. . . . It was the duty of the Israelites to retain him within their Commonwealth, though the master should have pursued him even to their very gates. God has forbidden his delivery.

Mitchell's book blasted owners of human beings, northerners who promoted their interests, ministers who justified bondage, and government officials who enforced slaveholder laws. His own position appeared in the words of an indignant former

An abolitionist depiction of a fugitive being seized by a posse

slave, who said, "It is slavery I hate and not my owners."[2]

Mitchell was highly critical of many northern whites:

> The North, in many respects, does the bidding of the South; they are the Slave-hunters for their masters, the Slave-holders.
>
> The North supports slavery, both in Church and State. . . . men in the Northern states who own Slaves in the South; merchants in New York, Boston, Philadelphia, (but especially New York) who have mortgages on Slave Plantations in the South.[3]

Mitchell did more than reveal some of the secrets and perils of his profession. He celebrated its conductors as "patriotic men, white and colored, voluntarily going into the Slave States and bringing away their fellow men. . . . A personal friend of mine is now in prison for ninety and nine years, in the State of Kentucky, for leading away eight Slaves, being caught within the limits of that State."

His stories also provide insights into the wit and wisdom he and other conductors employed. Soon after a runaway reached his house, it was surrounded by a posse. Mitchell demanded a warrant from the mayor and, as the posse rode off for it, Mitchell's wife dressed the fugitive "in her own attire, and in a few minutes he was transformed into the image of a female." Mitchell opened the door for his wife and the new woman and "the supposed ladies passed out." Mrs. Mitchell led the man to a conductor miles away. That evening he crossed into Canada.

When the posse returned to search his house, Mitchell, holding his eighteen-month-old crying baby in his arms, warned them "in a commanding tone" not to disturb his furniture. "This brought everything to a perfect stand still and dead silence: all their eyes were placed on me, and mine were placed on them; the cries of my child only served to augment my determination."[4]

Mitchell describes a fugitive who was turned in by a Cincinnati fortune-teller. At the courthouse "there was no possible chance of saving him by law, so we made as great a noise about it as possible, to awaken sympathy, and a proper sense of justice in the public mind." On the Saturday of the trial, the court was filled with people of both colors, attorneys argued heatedly, and the audience became unruly. At this point a friend of Mitchell placed his hat on the prisoner, who dropped to the floor unnoticed and then crawled through the crowd. The sheriff, suddenly finding his prisoner had left, offered a one thousand-dollar reward for his recapture. On Sunday Mitchell and other conductors dressed the prisoner in women's clothing and brought him to church, where money was collected to facilitate his escape to Canada.[5]

In a section of Ohio he does not name where he established a station, William Mitchell "witnessed remarkable specimens of heroism" from John Mason, who had escaped Kentucky. Five years later, Mason returned to aid others.

> This slave brought to my house, in 19 months, 265 human beings, whom he had been instrumental in redeeming from slavery; all of whom I had the privilege of forwarding to Canada . . . . He kept no record as to the number he had assisted in this way. I have only been able, from conversations with him on the subject, to ascertain about 1,300 whom he delivered to abolitionists to be forwarded to Canada. Poor man, he was finally captured and sold.

Mitchell's book also argued for equality that rested on universal humanity: "the Negro is as capable of loving and hating to the same degree as any other race of people. They that think to the contrary, are either prejudiced against the race, or ignorant of human nature."[6]

John P. Parker

In 1827 John P. Parker was born into slavery in Norfolk, Virginia. He remembered the brutality of slavery and some of its gentler moments before he purchased his freedom for $1,800 in 1845 by using his iron-foundry skills.[7]

Parker left to settle in Cincinnati, where he married Miranda Boulden. In 1849 the couple moved to Ripley, on the Ohio River across from Kentucky and only fifty-five miles southeast of Cincinnati. Ripley, home to many antislavery figures, had a distinctly abolitionist flavor. Its antislavery society claimed three hundred members, and Ripley's sentiments were also shaped by two nearby Black towns.

Early in Ohio history Ripley became a mecca for former slaves, and also former owners who were opposed to slavery. For example, in 1803 Alexander Campbell arrived in town and freed his slaves; later he served in the Ohio legislature and the U.S. Senate, and in 1835 became the vice president of the first Ohio Anti-slavery Society. In 1797 another white man, Obed Denham, left Virginia and founded Bethel, Ohio, west of Ripley, where he endowed a Baptist church for people "who do not hold slaves" or even "commune . . . with those that do practice such tyranny over their fellow creatures." William Dunlop also freed his slaves and settled them in Ripley.[8]

One of the town's most influential figures was the Reverend James Gilliland, a white man reared in South Carolina and educated at Dickinson College in Pennsylvania. In 1796 he was charged with political treason for preaching against bondage in South Carolina, and the Presbyterian synod forbade him to speak on the subject. In 1805 he moved to Ohio, where for thirty-nine years he directed the Red Oak Church and opened other churches at Ripley, Decatur, Russelville, and Georgetown "for repentant slaveholders," he said.[9]

The Reverend Samuel Doak was a Princeton graduate who preached in Virginia and North Carolina, and in 1795 founded Washington College, where he served as president until 1818. Doak freed his slaves, settled with them in Ohio, and trained young ministers in antislavery principles.

In the 1820s the Reverend John Rankin, Doak's son-in-law, moved to Ripley, served as pastor of the Presbyterian church for forty-seven years, and became a noted community leader. Rankin converted his two-story brick home overlooking the Ohio River into an Underground Railroad station. John Parker described Rankin as "a man of deeds as well as words" who with his six sons commanded "their border castle against all comers." "A lighted candle stood as beacon which could be seen from across the river, and like the north star was the guide to the fleeing slave."[10]

Because Rankin's family fed and aided many fugitives, proslavery Kentuckians often beseiged his home and even offered rewards of $2,500 for his capture, dead or alive. But he was a man not easily deterred. The Rankin house, called Liberty Hill, is today an Ohio landmark, open to the public with its "staircase to liberty."[11]

It was Rankin who welcomed John Parker when he moved to Ripley. In Ripley, he continued his trade as an ironworker and set up his home as a station on the railroad. He sped fugitives a few miles northward to James Gilliland's station at Red Oak, which was perhaps the largest in the country.

Home of conductor John P. Parker in Ripley, Ohio

From 1849 through the Civil War years, Parker was an active conductor, and at the same time he opened his home to fugitives. Though it could have meant his own arrest or even death, he repeatedly crossed into Kentucky to help escapees. He recalled a violent and terrible era for Ripley:

> There was a time . . . when fierce passions swept this little town, dividing its people into bitter factions. I never thought of going uptown without a pistol in my pocket, a knife in my belt, and a blackjack handy. Day or night I dared not walk on the sidewalks for fear someone might leap out of a narrow alley at me.[12]

Parker was hardly alone: "What I did other men did, walked

the streets armed." He spoke of incidents in which "pursuers and pursued stood at bay in a narrow alley with pistols drawn, ready for the assault," "angry men surrounded" houses and "kept up gunfire until late in the afternoon . . . in search of runaways." At night "the uncertain steps of slaves were heard quietly seeking their friends" and men with knives and pistols "used them on the least provocation." It was a fearful time, since much depended on him and his family.

> I am now living under my own roof, which still stands just as it did in the old strange days. I saw it grow brick by brick. It too has heard the gentle tapping of fugitives. It also has heard the cursing at the door of angry masters. It too has played its part in concealing men and women seeking a haven of safety. . . . we have seen adventurous nights together. . . .[13]

Parker described the inner strength of many of those whom he assisted in their flight.

> Men and women whom I helped on their way came from Tennessee, requiring weeks to make the journey, sleeping under the trees in the daytime and slowly picking their dangerous way at night. How they crossed the numerous creeks that lay waiting for them like a trap was unbelievable to me. As a matter of fact, they became backwoodsmen, following the north star, or even mountains, to reach their destination, the Ohio river. . . .
>
> These long-distance travelers were usually people strong physically, as well as people of character, and were resourceful when confronted with trouble, otherwise they could have never escaped.[14]

When Parker died, the *Cincinnati Commercial Tribune* said "a more fearless creature never lived. He gloried in danger. . . . He would go boldly over into the enemy's camp and filch the fugitives to freedom."[15]

By the 1840s Ohio was no longer a frontier, a borderland between advancing European settlements and retreating Native Americans. Farms dotted the landscape, and newspapers brought news to every corner of the state.[16]

In 1849 the Western Anti-Slavery Society meeting expressed "cause for joy and exultation in the escape of so many slaves from their prison house, and in the change of public opinion" which they believed made "the fugitive bondman comparatively safe from his blood thirsty pursuers."[17]

Henry Bibb

Former Kentucky slave Henry Bibb made his name as a voice who urged African Americans to leave the United States for Canada. In 1815 he was born into slavery on the plantation of Willard Gatewood in Shelby County, Kentucky. James Bibb, his father, was a state senator and the owner of Mildred Jackson, Henry's mother. Henry grew up with light skin and straight hair.

Though the Bibbs were spared hard work and painful punishments, the young man saw bondage destroying his family. Mrs. Jackson married a Black boatman, who asked Gatewood to free his wife. The two men signed an agreement, only to have Gatewood change his mind. Young Henry also saw his sisters and brothers sold away one at a time.

A fugitive couple fights off hounds sent after them. [Moorland-Springarn Research Center, Howard University]

In his teens, Bibb married Malinda, a light-skinned slave, and they soon had a child, Mary Frances. Bibb began to plot an escape, and in 1837 he fled to Cincinnati. The following year, wearing false whiskers, he returned for Malinda and Mary Frances, only to be recaptured.[18]

Bibb carried out daring escapes under six different owners, but was recaptured each time he returned for his family. In 1840, his owner, tired of his flights, sold Bibb but not his wife to slave traders. As Malinda wailed, he was led away, never to see his wife or daughter again.

In 1842, Bibb finally escaped to Canada. He returned to the
United States to attend a Detroit school and began to meet
some of the city's antislavery advocates. He began to attend
abolitionist meetings, and in 1844 in Michigan, he gave his first
antislavery speech. He was recruited for a tour through rural
Ohio and Michigan addressing white farm families who traveled in oxcarts to hear him. He wrote:

> Our meetings were generally in small log cabins,
> schoolhouses, among the farmers.
>   The people were poor, and in many places not
> able to give us a decent night's lodging. We most
> generally carried a few pounds of candles to light
> up the houses where we held our meetings after
> night; for in many places they had neither candles
> nor candlesticks.
>   I traveled for miles over swamps, where the roads
> were covered with logs, which sometimes shook and
> jostled the wagon to pieces. We would have to tie it
> up with bark, or take the lines to tie it with and lead
> the horse by the bridle. At times we were in mud up
> to the hubs of the wheels.[19]

Two of Bibb's white friends, a minister and a cabinetmaker,
had agreed to travel through Kentucky searching for his wife
and child. In 1845, he heard the news that his wife had remar-
ried, but he was able—"with unspeakable joy"—to find his
mother.[20]

For five years Bibb's masterful, dramatic antislavery lectures
laced painful experience with humor and pathos. From New
York and Massachusetts to Michigan, his earnest tales deeply
affected audiences. When he delivered "the mother's lament," a
lyrical song about people about to be sold from their families,
people gasped and some cried. A journalist described a Bibb
audience that "cheered, clapped, stamped, laughed, and wept,
by turns."[21]

At a New York City conference, Bibb met and fell in love with
Mary Miles, whose "principles and my own were nearly one and
the same." The couple were married in 1848, and the following

NARRATIVE

OF THE

LIFE AND ADVENTURES

OF

HENRY BIBB,

AN AMERICAN SLAVE.

WRITTEN BY HIMSELF.

WITH

AN INTRODUCTION

BY LUCIUS C. MATLACK.

THIRD STEREOTYPE EDITION.

NEW YORK:
PUBLISHED BY THE AUTHOR, 5 SPRUCE STREET.
1849.

In 1849 Henry Bibb published his slave narrative

year he wrote his autobiography, *Narrative of the Life and Adventures of Henry Bibb, an American Slave.*

One of the best of more than a hundred firsthand testimonies to appear during the slave era, the goal of the *Narrative of the Life and Adventures of Henry Bibb, an American Slave* was "to leave my humble testimony on record against this man-destroying system." He provided rich details of an inhuman system. He described running away for the first time in 1835 after being whipped by a woman with an uncontrollable temper. He told how slaveholders "look with utter contempt" on laborers of any color. A white Boston paper stated that no one who read his story would ever favor human bondage.

The 1850 Fugitive Slave Law allowed southern posses to roam the North to capture escaped slaves. No person of color was safe. Since Bibb's biography revealed that he was a fugitive, under the new law he could be legally arrested and returned to bondage. His first response was to join other African American leaders in urging massive resistance. He said: "If there is no alternative but to go back to slavery, or die contending for liberty, then death is far preferable."

Henry and Mary Bibb were among those fugitives who decided to settle in Canada to escape recapture. In the first three months after the passage of the Fugitive Slave Law, an estimated three thousand African American men, women, and children crossed into Canada, and by 1860 another twelve thousand had entered. In Chatham, Ontario, the Bibbs joined a pioneer Black community and helped it establish a school and a Methodist church. Soon there were antislavery, temperance, and educational societies in Chatham, Sandwich, and Windsor.

Then, on January 1, 1850, in Windsor, Henry Bibb published the first issue of his *Voice of the Fugitive,* the first newspaper issued by Canada's people of African descent. Published every two weeks, it celebrated the battle for freedom and justice in the United States through essays by leading abolitionists such as Frederick Douglass, Samuel Ringgold Ward, Sojourner Truth, William Lloyd Garrison, Wendell Phillips, and Joshua Giddings. The next year Bibb had a coeditor, writer Theodore Holly, who arrived in Windsor with his new bride, Charlotte.[22]

Holly had been a consistent advocate for a Black exodus from the United States. He and Bibb wrote a clarion call for African Americans to leave for Canada, "where all men are free." Their *Voice of the Fugitive* extolled Canada's favorable climate, crops, and job openings. They hoped to start an African American flight from the United States, and personally appeared at border crossings to greet new arrivals. Though thousands left for Canada, the numbers never amounted to the huge exodus Bibb and Holly sought.

Bibb was also able to welcome his mother, and then his brothers, John, Lewis, and Granville, to his Canadian home. Once his family had been largely reunited, Bibb crossed into Michigan and began a tour that raised enough money to purchase two thousand acres of land for a Refuge Home Society near Windsor.

The editors of the *Voice of the Fugitive* hammered away at the message that overthrowing U.S. slavery was hopeless, and the time to depart had arrived. In September 1851, Bibb and Holly organized the North American Convention of Colored People, which condemned the Fugitive Slave Act and urged free people to abandon the United States for the free soil of Canada. To promote emigration, convention delegates formed the American Continental and West India League.[23]

Bibb was only thirty-nine in 1854, when he died in Canada. Theodore Holly never stopped espousing emigration and in 1856 he became a minister of the Protestant Episcopal Church. However, Holly shifted his destination from Canada to Haiti after he had explored that Caribbean country and negotiated a treaty that granted his followers building sites. No treaty had been signed, but Holly returned to tell U.S. audiences that Haiti awaited them. Holly was unsuccessful in receiving U.S. government aid for his exodus, but he was made a recruiting agent by the Haitian government. He had planted a seed, but since few people were willing to leave the land of their birth, and fewer still had the money to reach Haiti, little came of his efforts.

chapter 7

The Malvins of Cleveland

*"Fifty years of struggle in Ohio on behalf of the American
slave and the equal rights of man."*

Cleveland, separated from Canada by Lake Erie, became a log-
ical destination for fugitives seeking to flee the country. The earliest fugitives arrived in 1799, before the region was opened to
settlement. By 1815 runaways often found hiding places aboard
schooners anchored at the foot of Superior Street. Conductors
brought men, women, and children through Underground Railroad stations that started in Medina, Ohio, in the south and in
Norwalk in the southwest.[1]

In 1831, when the Malvins arrived in Cleveland with high
hopes and little else, they found a pleasant town with 1,100 citizens, four churches, two dozen busy saloons, high prices, and
fewer than a hundred other African American residents.

Over the next twenty years Cleveland's population soared to
17,000, but this included only 224 people of color. White residents did not consider this small number a threat and raised no
heavy hand against their progress. In this, Cleveland was unlike
Cincinnati and other cities of the Northwest Territory with
larger Black populations.[2]

John Malvin, destined to become a leading citizen of Cleveland, was born in 1795 in Virginia to Dalcus Malvin, a free
Prince William County woman, and a man enslaved to a
wealthy planter. From age seven to eleven John was employed
as a personal servant to a clerk and served meals to and worked
among the field hands. He "observed the miseries of slavery"
and as a free man suffered almost as badly:

Though I was an apprentice, I was treated little better than a slave myself. I was supplied every year
with one pair of shoes, two pairs of linen pantaloons, one pair of cotton pantaloons, and a negro
cotton round jacket. My food consisted of one peck
of corn meal a week. Sometimes I received a supply
of salt. . . . I was obliged to other means to obtain
food.

Working alongside his father, Malvin was trained in the carpenter's trade. After watching others who could read, he "became possessed of a desire to learn to read." At night an old
slave with a Bible secretly instructed him: "We did not dare to
talk loud, lest we should be overheard, and had to confine ourselves to whispers. Such was the means and circumstances
under which I learned to read and spell."

Malvin lived with his parents in Virginia, though he had
begun to preach and tried to read "every opportunity I could
get . . . whenever I could obtain a paper or book." Then at
thirty-three, seized by "a spirit of adventure," he received his
proof of freedom from a state court and left Virginia bearing
nothing but his freedom papers and an extra shirt.

It took six days for Malvin to walk across the Blue Ridge
Mountains and follow the Shenandoah River to Marietta, Ohio.
Then he took a flatboat to Cincinnati. He was surprised by what
he found: "I thought upon coming to a free state like Ohio, that
I would find every door thrown open to me, but from the treatment I received by the people generally, I found it little better
than Virginia." William Jay, son of the first chief justice of the
U.S. Supreme Court, wrote of the Ohio Valley: "Prejudice
against the Negro attains its rankest luxuriance, not in the
swamps of Georgia, nor the sugar-fields of Louisiana but upon
the prairies of Ohio."

Ohio's Black Laws denied Malvin the right to vote, serve on
a jury, testify in court, serve in the militia, or make use of "any
of the institutions of this State." He said: "I found every door
closed against the colored man in a free state, excepting the
jails and penitentiaries, the doors of which were thrown wide
open to receive him." In 1850, Ohio jailed less than 2 percent

of its whites and 17 percent of its Black people.

In Cincinnati, Malvin began a society of citizens of color seeking a place "where we could be on an equal social footing." The group purchased thirty thousand acres in Canada and established the Wilberforce colony (named after a noted English abolitionist) as a home for 460 Black exiles from Ohio.[3]

But John Malvin was not drawn to this distant refuge and remained in Cincinnati, where he next entered into the dangerous job of aiding escapees. He began one night when he helped a pregnant friend of his mother and her son escape from a ship under the noses of two sentries. Mother and son found hiding places in town and then were sent on to Canada. Malvin next freed two men and a woman and sent them westward to Indiana.[4]

In March 1829 Malvin married Miss Harriet Dorsey in Cincinnati, but in five months the couple moved to Louisville, Kentucky, then to Middletown, where they worked for the owner of his wife's enslaved father, Caleb Dorsey, as Mrs. Malvin did not want to leave her father. Although a freeman, Malvin was arrested as a runaway, handcuffed, stripped, and threatened with a whip if he did not confess. Though he defied his captors, he was not whipped, and finally produced three hundred dollars in bail. But John Malvin had had enough of Kentucky.

Harriet remained in Louisville near her father while John left for Canada and purchased a farm. In 1831 the Malvins finally left Kentucky for Canada, passed through Cleveland, and reached Buffalo, New York. At that point, Harriet refused to go on. She said she could not leave her enslaved father. In an age when men dictated all crucial decisions, the couple wrestled with a hard choice. Malvin later described this moment of pain, trial, and decision:

> It lay so heavily upon her that she gave me no rest. Seeing her unwillingness to go to Canada, and her fears that she would never see her father again, I concluded to give up the farm, and my wife having taken a fancy to Cleveland, was determined to go back and settle there.[5]

Settled in Cleveland, John Malvin took a cook's job on a schooner, and the couple began to save money to purchase Mr. Dorsey, who was sixty. Then Mrs. Malvin left for Kentucky with one hundred dollars down and promissory notes. She alone would negotiate her father's release from Mr. Hudson, his owner. Malvin described the couple's decision in these words: "I sent my wife to Kentucky with the money and notes, and on paying the $100.00 and delivering the notes, her father was released, and came with her to Cleveland." One wonders if the strong-willed woman who "gave her husband no rest" on the issue had simply decided to make the trip on her own.

Mr. Dorsey was also proven a man of independent mind. After fifteen years sawing wood in Cleveland, he decided to visit his children who were still enslaved in Louisville. At seventy-five, he waved aside the Malvins' objections and arrived in Louisville on a Saturday. He attended church Sunday morning with his children, and that night caught cholera and died.

In 1832 the Malvins lived at Hamilton and Wood Streets on the eastern edge of the city, in the heart of what was to become Cleveland's mall. They later resided on York street, Cedar Avenue, and then on Sterling Street.

Over the decades John and Harriet Malvin helped launch many campaigns for justice in Cleveland, he publicly and she behind the scenes. The couple organized the First Baptist Church and, in 1835, helped erect its first building on Seneca and Champlain Streets. He was asked on occasion to address the largely white congregation—and was pleased to do so.

But then the church elders announced plans to segregate its congregants of color in a balcony section, after first offering the Malvins seats among whites. Shocked at this segregation, Malvin, a direct, dignified, and optimistic man, said, "If I had to be colonized, I preferred to be colonized in Liberia, rather than the House of God; Christ or the Apostles never made any distinction on account of race or color."

With this blast of anger Harriet and John Malvin inaugurated Cleveland's earliest civil rights movement. For months the couple battled the church fathers and rejected compromise for total victory. After eighteen months, segregation at the First Baptist Church was ended. The campaign proved unique, a rare defeat over racism in the Northwest Territory.[6]

As the Malvins voiced their opposition to the Black Laws, their personal victory and courage fueled a host of other community-led activities. Their example insured that African Americans would provide the struggle's leadership and determine its methods and goals. To campaign for equality in Ohio, the Malvins launched conventions, started petition drives, and held endless meetings. African Americans, an Ohio scholar wrote, "sparked by Malvin among others, learned how to organize and act as a coherent interest group."[7]

The Malvins' victory at the First Baptist Church led to similar efforts to win open seating in other churches. This defeat of church segregation in Cleveland spelled doom there for independent African American congregations that thrived elsewhere. Members of St. John's African Methodist Episcopal Church, founded in 1830, took eighteen years to build a permanent home, and only attracted former slaves who felt uncomfortable worshiping among affluent white parishioners. Each Sunday Black people sat next to whites in church, but the price of this was that no Black church sank its roots into Cleveland's soil.[8]

In 1832 the Malvins joined with other African Americans to organize a community school to secure a decent education for African American children despite Ohio's school law denying them admission. It began with a male teacher hired for twenty dollars a month, and then other instructors of both sexes.

In 1835 John Malvin was among Ohioans who called a statewide African American convention in Columbus primarily aimed at opening the public schools to Black children. The delegates failed to move Ohio's legislators, but their new School Fund Society soon built educational facilities in Cincinnati, Columbus, Springfield, and Cleveland. Classes also were attended by adults who had never been taught to read or write. Malvin and others next mobilized a petition drive to desegregate the city schools.[9]

In the 1840s and 1850s Malvin helped his people organize seven state conventions to protest the Black Laws. The 1849 convention in Columbus brought forty-one delegates from twelve counties.[10]

In 1831, when the couple first arrived, Malvin could not get a job as a carpenter, but by 1839 Cleveland counted a large number of successful Black entrepreneurs, skilled artisans, and tradesmen, carpenters, masons, blacksmiths, and canal boat captains. That year the *Cleveland Herald* said of this rising middle class: "They are industrious, peaceable, intelligent and ambitious of improvement."[11]

In 1841 a white meeting to support the Black Laws called African Americans innately inferior, unable to earn "an honest living," and likely to associate with criminals. In other cities such words could stimulate white violence, but not among Cleveland's white population.

Cleveland's African American middle class grew in numbers and respect. In 1858, the *Cleveland Leader* characterized this class of African Americans as "old, intelligent, industrious and respectable citizens, who own property, pay taxes, vote at elections, educate their children in public schools, and contribute to build up the institutions and to the advancement of the prosperity of the city." In 1859 a sympathetic white, James F. Clarke, said: "There you find them master carpenters, master painters, shopkeepers, and growing rich every year." They were also barbers, inventors, manufacturers, teachers, and a college-educated doctor."[12]

Black residents of Cleveland found less prejudice and greater opportunities than their sisters and brothers in other Ohio cities.

The Malvins helped to generate white support for equal justice in

John Mercer Langston graduated from Oberlin College in 1849 and three years later earned a master's degree there. He became an attorney and a leading civil rights advocate. [Library of Congress]

Cleveland and from 1834 to 1838 Ohio's abolitionist societies multiplied from twelve to over three hundred. Antislavery groups, an eyewitness reported, started their work "amid the crashing of stones against doors and windows, and the hootings of a mob." Undeterred by mobs, more abolitionist societies sprouted in Ohio than in any other state.[13]

In 1847 Frederick Douglass and William Lloyd Garrison barnstormed through central Ohio accompanied some of the time by abolitionists Martin R. Delany and Lucretia and James Mott. In town after town Garrison found "the enthusiasm of our friends, out here, is glorious. They cannot wait for our arrival into their towns, but come ten, twenty, thirty and even forty miles, with their own teams, to meet us."[14]

Garrison and Douglass addressed crowds in Medina, Richfield, Massillon, Leesburgh, Salem, New Lisbon, Ravenna, Warren, and finally in Cleveland, where Malvin joined them at a public meeting. Garrison's letters tell of enthusiastic receptions and large audiences.[15]

In 1849, after years of black agitation, the Ohio legislature repealed the Black Laws. Repeal was fashioned from a deal that ended a political deadlock among the Democratic, Whig, and Free Soil Parties.[16]

By 1850 the Malvins had taken an active part in virtually all of Ohio's antislavery and civil rights activities. John Malvin assisted in the legal defense of captured runaways, and provided bail money for penniless African Americans "in order that they might have a fair opportunity to prepare for trial and test the truth of the charge" against them. Malvin was not a man to suffer lies and fraud from anyone, however, as Archey Lorton, arrested in 1856 as a horse thief, found out after Malvin provided his bail. When Lorton fled to Canada rather than face trial, an irate Malvin

Antislavery voice William Lloyd Garrison found a warm welcome in Ohio and addressed crowds with John Malvin in Cleveland.

pursued and argued unsuccessfully before Canadian courts for his extradition. But when Lorton committed a crime in Canada years later and fled to Michigan, Malvin helped secure his arrest and a conviction that sent the horse thief to prison for seven years.[17]

A fugitive slave dictates his story so the public can learn the horrors of human bondage.

When African American churches in Cleveland proved too weak to lead civil rights struggles, Malvin helped his community develop secular groups. One of these, formed in 1839, was the Young Men's Union Society, whose purpose was to promote reading and debating "in order that we may become good and virtuous citizens and not be a disgrace to our country by our ignorance."

In the 1850s an African American theater company with its own playwright produced topical dramas. Two years later the Black Masons organized a society, and the Odd Fellows organization three years after that. And that same year a Black volunteer militia troop marched in the first West Indian Independence Day festivities on August 1.[18]

Ohio also became a fertile ground for new African American ideas of equality. In 1849, only a year after the first Women's Rights Convention in Seneca Falls, New York, launched white women's drive for political equality, Black women threatened a boycott at a Black Ohio state convention. Women were invited to speak at a convention of African American men assembled in 1856 in Columbus.

The Malvin family effort for Ohio never slowed. They continued to found and support civil rights groups and raise funds for the Ohio Anti-Slavery Society. John spoke at August 1 West Indian emancipation celebrations, and lectured alone or alongside Frederick Douglass.

From the time of his arrival in Cleveland, Malvin was able to bring older agitators for the cause together with a new generation he had inspired. He often worked with an activist named John Brown, who in 1828 left Virginia for Cleveland and became a barber and local philosopher. His investments in real estate created an estate worth almost forty thousand dollars and provided the confidence and wealth to confront his people's foes. Brown soon became a staunch, independent-minded, quarrelsome early voice for his people. Brown and Malvin were among Cleveland's few people of color with the ready cash to bail out those unjustly snared in legal nets.

John A. Copeland attended Oberlin College, aided fugitive slaves in Ohio, and in 1859 was captured with John Brown at Harpers Ferry. "I am dying for freedom!" he shouted before he was hanged.

Brown's stepson, William H. Day, was also a leading Cleveland activist. Born in 1825 to a wealthy New York family, he loved to read and at age sixteen excelled at Latin and Greek. He was educated in private schools, learned to be a printer, and entered Oberlin College at seventeen. He used his skills as a printer to pay tuition, and graduated in 1847 the only African American in a class of fifty. Five years later the studious young agitator married Lucia Station, another Oberlin graduate, and the couple moved to Cleveland to devote their lives to uplifting their people.[19]

In 1848, Day was instrumental in bringing to Cleveland, and served as chairman of, a National Convention of Colored Freemen, which had Frederick Douglass as president. In 1849 African Americans selected Day to address the Ohio legislature. He was on his way to becoming Ohio's voice for the political and educational rights of his people. Malvin chose Day as one of several lecturers to tour the state, demanding repeal of the Black Laws.

In 1852, after Day had assembled the remaining Black veterans of the War of 1812 for a celebration, he was made the orator of the day. In 1853 Day and Samuel R. Ward served as coeditors of the *Aliened American* weekly, the first Black weekly newspaper in the Ohio Valley. Its first issue of April 9, 1853, printed a long report on the January Ohio Convention of Colored Freemen.[20]

When the *Aliened American* paper folded, Day began another paper advocating abolition and full citizenship rights. The *Rising Sun* lauded Day's scholarship and editorial talents, and concluded that "as a speaker and writer, he has done much for his race."[21]

Day also worked on the staff of the white *Daily True Democrat,* but in 1854 was expelled from the Ohio Senate's press gallery because of his color. That year he also served as a librarian for the white Cleveland Library Association, where he worked so hard his health deteriorated. Day left for a rest in Canada but quickly neglected his recuperation as he set about to help U.S. fugitive slaves.

To aid Black Canadians, Day left for a fund-raising tour of England, Ireland, and Scotland, where he addressed enthusiastic audiences. He spoke to the General Assembly of Ireland's Presbyterian Church, and throughout Europe raised an astonishing thirty-five thousand dollars to finance a church and school in Canada.

Day met with the fiery white antislavery crusader John Brown, and was given the secret job of printing a constitution for the multiracial republic Brown planned following his 1859 raid at Harpers Ferry. Day also helped form an African Aid Society and encouraged editor and nationalist Martin Delany to explore Africa in search of a home for African Americans.[22]

During the Civil War, Day returned to the United States and addressed an Emancipation Meeting at Cooper Union in New York City. He was appointed to assist former slaves in Maryland and Delaware, and his labors resulted in the founding of 140 schools and the hiring of 150 teachers to serve 7,000 students. In Delaware he also organized Black voters. Day lived until 1900 and became a preacher in the AME Zion Church.

Changes came to Cleveland during the Civil War. A local paper boasted that "colored children attend all our public schools, and colored people are permitted to attend all public lectures and public affairs . . . and no one is offended."[23]

Malvin, Day, and other activists had achieved their share of victories over bigotry, but even their efforts had not ended Cleveland's color line. Until 1870, Black people could not serve on Cleveland juries. The Academy of Music still only seated Black patrons in the balcony, and streetcars remained segregated. The legal system improved somewhat, but still a city justice system convicted and jailed people of color, but did not send white people to prison for the same crimes. People of color were punished far more severely for committing crimes against whites than against other African Americans.[24]

After the Civil War Malvin became a distinguished son of Ohio, a noted Republican speaker, and a man white newspapers said had served the cause of humanity and "who has labored hard for the elevation of the colored race."

In 1879 Malvin finished his autobiography, an optimistic work he called "an authentic account of 50 years of struggle in Ohio in behalf of the American slave and the equal rights of all men." He died the next year at the age of eighty-five. His wife's death is not recorded.[25]

The *Cleveland Leader* eulogized him as a "Noble and Worthy Man Whose Thoughts Were of His People." When Julia Foote, a former slave who became an evangelist, said, "I shall praise God through all eternity for sending me to Cleveland," she also should have thanked the Malvins.[26]

chapter 8

The Fight for Liberty in Indiana

"After having inflicted such monstrous and inhuman out-rages upon us, they tell us, tauntingly, that we are an inferior race."

In 1702 people of African descent were present when Indiana's oldest town, Vincennes, was founded by French trappers on the lower Wabash River. Black people built the fortifications that made Vincennes one of France's key outposts in the New World. By 1746 its population stood at five enslaved Africans and forty French trappers and missionaries. Several years later the St. Francis Xavier Catholic Church began to record the births, marriages, and deaths of its African residents.[1]

In some states, free Black people who were jailed and could not pay their fines could be sold into slavery.

In the late eighteenth century most pioneers entering the area that was to become the Indiana Territory were northerners pleased that the Northwest Ordinance had banned slavery. However, they soon discovered that, as in Ohio, slaveholders and their friends held political power, particularly in the southern part of the territory.

In 1796 land speculators in what was to become Indiana Territory insisted that they spoke for a majority when they petitioned Congress to permit slavery as an economic boon to the region. Four years later speculators again forwarded a petition to the U.S. Senate signed by 277 Indiana citizens requesting a legal right to enslave Black men until age thirty-one and Black women until age twenty-eight.[2]

Soon after 1800, when Indiana became a territory, its legislature received five petitions calling for slavery's restoration. The requests were refused, but only because legislators feared a violation of the Northwest Ordinance could lead to their being denied admission as a state.

In 1803, Indiana legislators approved a legal fiction called "indenture" that actually permitted slavery. By calling slaves "indentured servants" and having them mark an X on a legal document, owners were legally able to enter Indiana with slaves. Masters compelled enslaved people to sign agreements of indenture that committed them to work from twenty to forty years.[3]

From 1801 to 1813 Indiana's first territorial governor, General William Henry Harrison, brought his Kentucky slaves into Indiana as indentured servants. "Thirty days after her arrival" in Indiana he made one slave, Molly, into an indentured servant. In a letter to a friend he worried "if she refuses to indent herself" he might "lose her service." Did this mean that he thought Molly had an independent mind and might refuse to sign an indenture agreement? Harrison later served as a congressman, a senator, and as president of the United States.

In 1813 a new governor, Thomas Posey, a Virginia planter, claimed he "had disposed of what few [slaves] I had." However, in 1816 he willed two slaves to his children.[4]

Though Indiana's indenture law was repealed in 1810, state officials allowed masters to continue to hold people as indentured servants or even slaves. That year's census listed 630 African Americans in the Indiana Territory: 237 were "slaves" and many others were indentured servants. An 1813 bill of sale showed that one woman, Dinah, age seventeen, was sold for $371, and the next year a white man paid $550 for a Kentucky woman who remained his indentured servant for many years.

The first battle facing African Americans in Indiana was to break free of the slavery that paraded as indenture. Many appealed to the legal system for justice. In 1816 Lydia, whose mother had been indentured in Indiana, won a long struggle for freedom in Kentucky. Even though she was sold three times, she carried her case to Kentucky's Supreme Court. The court ruled that she was a free woman since her mother was not a slave but an indentured servant.

Other African Americans initiated suits for liberty. A woman took her Kentucky master to court in Indiana for assault, battery, and false imprisonment. He produced her signed indenture promising to serve him until age fifty-two, but a white jury agreed she had been coerced, and awarded her fourteen dollars. In 1811, when an African American man sued his master saying his indenture had expired and he was held illegally, the court freed him. When a woman sued to break her indenture contract a judge also freed her.[5]

After Indiana entered the Union with a constitution that forbade bondage, suits by African Americans increased. Some fifteen African Americans brought seven different legal actions but lost in each case except one. In 1819 attorney Amory Kinney was asked by a woman named Polly to help liberate her from the Lasalles, one of Vincennes's leading French families. Kinney and Polly brought suit, lost, and then won on appeal to the Indiana Supreme Court. The justices cited the new state constitution and declared that "slavery can have no existence in the State of Indiana." Polly next sued her former master and won $25.16 in damages.

By 1820 court suits for liberty continued to increase, the phrase "indentured servant" no longer appeared in the census, and Indiana listed only 190 slaves. The next year four African Americans brought freedom suits before the state supreme court. In one, Mary Clark signed an indenture contract but sued her master anyway. Since Clark had "declared her will" and asked to be released from indenture, the high court ruled that this proved she was being held in bondage and it liberated her. By 1830 and largely through such efforts Vincennes's enslaved population fell to thirty-two.[6]

In 1803 Indiana's territorial legislature became the first to pass a law that banned African American testimony in courts. When the U.S. Congress did not object, Indiana legislators passed other Black Laws. In 1807, the territory prevented

African Americans from serving in the militia, and in 1811 it denied them the right to vote or to be elected to office. When
William Vincett of Kentucky brought forty-seven former slaves
to settle in Indiana, a white petition protested their arrival and
the legislature warned of "a holocaust." [7]

Indiana's Black Laws appeared designed to restrict the rights
of African Americans living in the state and to discourage further Black migration to the area. But they also accomplished a
far wider aim by driving off some early African American pioneers. In 1817 a white Vincennes man talked with Black settlers who now wanted to leave the Wabash area, and wrote this
report:

> There are, in this vicinity, between fifty and a hun-
> dred free people of colour, who . . . are desirous of
> going to Africa, to help in forming a settlement or
> colony, should one be attempted. They live on the
> Wabash, on both sides; some in Illinois territory, and
> some in Indiana. They are in general industrious and
> moral. Some of them have landed property and are
> good farmers; and some can read and write. They
> are sensible of the existing degraded condition in
> which they are placed by our laws, respecting the
> right of suffrage, and other disabilities. [8]

The threat of kidnapping also hung over Indiana's free people
of color, particularly those who settled near the Ohio River's

Kidnappers
enter a home
and seize a
mother and
child.
[Library of
Congress]

border with Kentucky. In Vincennes, Quaker William Forster learned about some family tragedies:

> We hear sad stories of kidnapping. I wish some active benevolent people would induce every person of colour to remove away from the river, as it gives wicked, unprincipled wretches the opportunity to get them into a boat, and carry them off to [New] Orleans or, where they still fetch a high price. I have been pleading hard with a black man and his wife to get off to some settlement of Friends, with their five children; and I hope they will go.[9]

In the same way, three men of color from Kentucky, freed in their master's will, settled in Indiana, only to be pursued by some of the master's heirs claiming ownership. An Indiana court ruled the three were free and issued an order preventing the Kentuckians from interfering with their lives.

Benjamin had a long record of resisting his Kentucky master. He refused to sign an indenture document and then convinced his owner to sell him his freedom. After gaining his freedom, he moved to Indiana, but his former master entered Indiana to seize him. Benjamin succeeded in bringing him to court, where a judge warned the Kentuckian to leave Benjamin alone.[10]

William Trail, a Maryland slave, was determined to find a free life in Indiana. He twice used forged passes to escape his master and twice he was recaptured before he won his freedom in court. In 1814, in Indiana, he cleared land for white farmers and saved enough money to buy himself 25 acres, on which he built a large home. In 1832 he purchased another 160 acres to build a new home.[11]

Despite Trail's wealth, the local school refused to admit his children. His older sons were educated elsewhere and returned home to conduct classes for their brothers and sisters and other children.

By 1838 some Black pioneers had become major landowners. In four Indiana counties, African Americans purchased 2,500 government acres and agreed to fell the trees and then farm the land.

In 1842 a white Quaker described the Black farmers at the Cabin Creek settlement as "capable of taking care of themselves if they have anything like a fair chance." By 1850 African American farming communities, some with Quaker help, flourished in many parts of Indiana: the Lyles' Station; the Roberts Settlement with some fifty members; the Weaver settlement; and the Bassett settlement.[12]

In southern states, the Society of Friends, or Quakers, played a key role in aiding many enslaved people to gain freedom, moving them to Indiana and helping them find jobs and education. In 1808, a North Carolina Quaker society reported that in six years it had helped more than 350 formerly enslaved people find liberty in Ohio. By 1830 these Quakers had helped 652 people reach free states.

Despite their actions some Quakers still accepted racial prejudice. One Indiana meeting decided: "Although it is desirable to avoid an excess of this class . . . as neighbors, we are concerned to impress it upon the minds of all, that our prejudices should yield when the interest and happiness of our fellow beings are at stake."

In 1821 Indiana Quakers appointed a committee on "the Concerns of People of Color" that operated for decades. Individual Quakers donated time and effort. In 1835 Quaker David White, at a cost of $2,490, sponsored a caravan of 135 Black men, women, and children who traveled to Indiana from North Carolina in 132 wagons and carts, together with donated clothing and food. Though four married women with children had to leave their enslaved husbands, Quakers later were able to purchase these men and reunite families. White left 4 people in Chillicothe, Ohio, 23 in Leesburg, Ohio, and 26 others in Newport, Indiana.

In 1849 a Quaker society reported of African Americans that "in country situations, they much more frequently become useful and moral citizens, than when employed in our cities and villages, as servants about hotels, etc." But many African Americans rejected rural life to take town jobs as porters and barbers, or on Ohio riverboats.

The 1850 Indiana census found that the state had 11,000 people of color. Of the 2,150 listed with an occupation, 976 were farmers and many others were farm laborers. Some 671 of these African Americans owned lands valued at $421,755, with some farms equal in size to those of prosperous whites. In 1855 African American William Shoemaker of South Carolina arrived in Indiana and bought 500 acres of land.[13]

In 1816 Jonathan Jennings, the first elected governor of the new state of Indiana, and a foe of slavery, had the legislature prohibit the kidnapping of free people. But in 1831, the state passed a law requiring a person of color who entered the state to post a bond for "good behavior." Though it was rarely enforced, it was one more law hanging over the lives of Black families in the state of Indiana.

In 1850, when delegates met to revise the Indiana Constitution, they voted 122 to 1 against granting suffrage to African Americans. Some delegates even refused to read suffrage petitions, and one delegate suggested that "all persons voting for negro suffrage shall themselves be disfranchised." One part of the constitution restricted voting to whites only and another section added this redundancy: "No negro or mulatto shall have the right of suffrage."

Delegates voted 93 to 40 for Article 13, which read: "No negro or mulatto shall come into, or settle in the State, after the adoption of this Constitution." Black residents, the constitution stated, had to register with local authorities. Any white person who hired an illegal migrant could be fined up to five hundred dollars, and contracts with illegal migrants were not enforceable.[14]

The white electorate endorsed Article 13 with a resounding 113,628-to-21,873 vote, and it carried all but four counties. In neighboring Illinois at this time, an exclusion provision also was enacted by a vote of 60,585 to 15,903.

Legislators wrote new Black Laws and made new threats. They denied African Americans the right to serve in the militia. Some called for a law denying African Americans the right to own real estate or sell land to other people of color. Delegates hoped this would drive people of color from the state. One delegate turned Black landholding into menace: "Let us, then, keep steadily in view the fact that [after all of Indiana land is owned] every negro freeholder necessarily excludes from the same land, some one of our own race."[15]

The legislature voted additional restrictions. In 1853 African American testimony was banned in state courts, and this prohibition was not removed until after the Civil War. Denied the right to testify, at least one pioneer decided to leave the state and stated his reason.

> I removed to Canada where I would have an equal oath with any man. Excepting for the oppressive laws, I would rather have remained in Indiana. I left one of the most beautiful places in the country. I had a two-story frame house, with piazza—good stable—abundance of apples, peaches, quinces, plums and grapes. I paid my taxes and felt hurt and angry too that I was not allowed my oath.[16]

Despite unfair laws, the threat of kidnapping, and bigoted neighbors, African American pioneers in Indiana tried to keep up their morale and inch ahead. For Independence Day, they chose not July 4, but August 1, when in 1833 slaves in the West Indies gained their freedom. Some also mobilized to challenge the menace of indenture regulations, kidnappings, and Black Laws. In 1843, 1847, and 1851 African Americans organized statewide protest conventions to discuss and present demands for citizenship rights and equality.

African American settlements had always welcomed a steady stream of runaway slaves. Escapees from Kentucky had fled to Indiana during its territorial days, and once they became settled these residents opened their homes to other escapees. African American communities formed along Indiana's main Underground Railroad lines.[17]

In 1826, when Quakers Levi and Sarah Coffin settled in New-

Fugitives receive help from Levi Coffin and his wife, Sarah (center), at their Indiana farm. [Library of Congress]

port, now Fountain City, help for runaways who reached Indiana began to accelerate. The Coffins discovered that their Black neighbors lacked the resources to help the many fugitives who passed through. So for the next twenty years the Coffins and African American conductors William Bush, Douglas White, Cal Thomas, William Davidson, and James Benson ran highly effective stations. Coffin reported:

> [T]he roads were always in good running order, the connections were good, the conductors active and zealous, and there was no lack of passengers. Seldom a week passed without our receiving passengers by this mysterious road. . . . We knew not what night or what hour of the night we would be roused from slumber by a gentle rap at the door.

The station was always busy, Coffin reported:

> I found it necessary to keep a team and wagon always at command, to convey the fugitive slaves on

their journey. Sometimes, when we had large companies, one or two teams and wagons were required. These journeys had to be made at night, often through deep mud and bad roads, and along byways that were seldom traveled.[18]

Three principal underground lines—from Cincinnati, from Madison, and from Jeffersonville—converged at the Coffin house. Levi Coffin became known as "the president of the Underground Railroad." Men, women, and children arrived destitute, hungry, without enough clothing, and sometimes barefoot. Often he and his wife found the fugitives were "afraid of every white person they saw."

This Eastman Johnson painting of 1862 shows a family fleeing slavery on their owner's horse.

From the Ohio River northward to Lake Michigan, Indiana's African American settlers mobilized to aid escapees. In 1839 the Reverend Chapman Harris and his wife arrived in Madison, Indiana, and opened a station, their four sons serving as conductors. The town's white hoodlums tried to force another conductor, Griffen Booth, to reveal his secrets. One time they beat him and a second time they threw him into the cold Ohio River, but he remained silent.

From his Black community outside of Hanover, Indiana, George Evans aided runaways who crossed the Ohio River on rafts. At Rockport in southeastern Indiana, Ben Swain's reward for aiding Kentucky runaways was a four-year sentence in a Kentucky jail. Oswald Wright of Corydon, Indiana, arrested for helping runaways, served five years in prison, and in 1857 Elijah Anderson, also arrested for aiding fugitives, died in the same prison.

By the 1840s African American resistance had spread northward from the Ohio River counties into many parts of Indiana. African American men formed armed militias, engaged in military training, and prepared to confront posses. Tennessee slave catchers rode into one county to seize two girls, only to be surrounded by people of color and their white friends. The girls made their escape.

In 1846, Sam, his wife, and their child—Kentucky runaways—worked on an Indiana farm as John and Louan Rhodes. When their master's posse tried to storm their barricaded cabin, the family fought back. The posse agreed to seek out a judge, and everyone rode off to court. But when a dispute erupted at a fork in the road, the friend driving the Rhodeses' wagon whipped his horses and rode off. The Rhodeses plunged into a swamp and raced off to liberty. Later they returned to live a peaceful life in Hamilton, Indiana.[19]

In a nearby county, in 1849, Kentucky slave hunters rode in, only to face an armed African American militia with many white supporters. Warned by the whites that no one "would leave town alive if they fired a pistol," the posse turned and rode off.[20]

That same year another Kentucky posse burst into a Black home and carried off a mother and her three sons. A county sheriff raced after the posse and handed the men a writ of habeas corpus. This forced the Kentuckians to prove their case before a judge in the town of South Bend. There the Kentuckians were confronted by angry Blacks and whites armed with clubs. In court, spectators snarled about freeing the prisoners, and the fearful posse clutched their knives and guns.

The next day even larger African American crowds appeared on the streets of South Bend. The slave hunters were arrested for assault and riot and faced a damage suit. Meanwhile, a judge dismissed charges against the alleged fugitives and they were hastened off to Michigan.

White sympathy for runaways did not mean that abolitionist speakers were

Frederick Douglass tries to fight off an Indiana mob.

Black children were denied admission to white schools in the free West and the East.

welcome in Indiana. In 1843 Frederick Douglass's antislavery campaign encountered Indiana mobs. "Sixty of the roughest characters" he ever saw "tore down the platform" at Pendleton, broke his hand, and left him bleeding and unconscious. But violence would not silence abolitionists in Indiana or elswhere.[21]

As in Ohio, educating their children became as important for many African American pioneer families as owning land or business success. From territorial days, however, Indiana denied Black children admission to public school. As in Ohio, when their children were kept out of white classrooms, African American parents built their own schools, hired teachers, and raised the money for books and supplies.

Black children were often taught in private homes until primitive classrooms, often in church buildings, could be found. These early schools operated only a few months a year and were conducted by young African American teachers. The curriculum included reading, writing, arithmetic, grammar, and geography.

One of the earliest Black Indiana schools opened in 1831 as a part of the Mount Pleasant Church. The community also created one of the first circulating libraries in the state, and from 1842 to 1867 the Mount Pleasant Library, part of the AME church, served both Black and white citizens. About sixty people paid a twenty-five-cent membership, which enabled them to read about ancient and U.S. history and religion. Library directors banned "Novels, Romances, or writings favourable to infidelity." Today a plaque on the church building notes that in 1832, four years after free people from North Carolina settled there, they chose the AME church "as their religious denomination."

Black schools also operated in four other Indiana counties and in Indianapolis, with instructors of both races and sexes.[22]

The most prominent Black teacher in Indiana was Samuel Smothers, who as a child had only attended school for nine months. A self-educated activist, he served as a director of the Union Literary Institute in Randolph County, and was also founder and editor of its periodical, the *Students' Repository*. Earlier, in 1845, four African Americans, aided by Quakers and other denominations, had founded the Union Literary Institute. A "school for all," it specifically invited children barred from other schools by racial bigotry.

Three years later, when the state issued the institute a charter as a manual training facility, it was situated on 180 acres of land and had an enrollment of fifty resident students twelve years and older who lived in a dormitory, and another group of mostly younger day students. Pupils, required to donate four hours of labor a day as part of their tuition, worked on farms, dug ditches, chopped wood, and constructed buildings. Discipline was strict and the sexes were separated. In 1850 enrollment stood at 131—92 boys and 39 girls—and 97 were African Americans.

Smothers was committed to education and repeal of the state's Black Laws. For him their worst feature was their denial of education to children. Championing his people's "rapidly rising talents and aspirations," Smothers challenged enemies who "struck down our liberties" and stifled "our manhood." He had sharp words for those who "sold us like beasts in the market" and "deprived us of education," and continued: "after having inflicted such monstrous and inhuman outrages upon us, they tell us, tauntingly, that we are an inferior race!"

In 1852 Indiana officially opened a public school system but denied admission to children of color. Though Indiana's Committee on Education spoke of "a duty to elevate" African American children, it feared integration would "degrade our own race." White educators said "blacks should be educated by some means" but said their attendance in public schools undermined learning.[23]

In 1846 a Wayne County school committee unanimously voted to admit Black children and pay their tuition. White parents who opposed their admission carried their case to the state supreme court. The justices upheld the parents and stated that African Americans were "unfit to associate" with whites.

Each refusal to educate their children brought a determined African American response. In 1847 delegates to an African American convention in Indianapolis demanded admission to schools. How can we be taxed for education and then denied it? they asked. In 1848 people of color in one county petitioned for school funds to maintain a separate school and were turned down. Two years later, Black apprentices were denied training in reading, writing, and arithmetic. But in 1855 a public school in Cabin Creek, Randolph County, was admitting children of color.

Agreeing that separate education was better than none, African Americans and their Quaker, Methodist, and Baptist friends often united to raise school funds. In 1840 the Indiana Society of Friends reported sponsorship of four schools with 309 pupils, and in 1852, there were nine schools with 632 African American pupils.

In 1855 Quakers at the Indiana Yearly Meeting announced their financial support of thirty schools for African American children, and in 1859 Quakers wholly operated fifteen schools. By 1860, through the efforts of parents and friends, a fourth of African American children in the state attended school. Most of these were run by Quakers or by Black communities who funded them totally or in part.

Though not much is known of the schools' curriculum or

teachers, one pupil wrote to his former teachers and classmates describing "the eight happy months I have spent with you in the pleasant schoolroom at Rich Square." Referring to his two female teachers, he said he was "cared for by our truly distinguished and well-known teachers . . .[and] shall ever feel myself under many obligations . . . for the kindness and respect they showed to me." [24]

INDIANA Territory 1800; State 1816

Population growth:

	1810	1820	1830	1840	1850	1860
Blacks	630	1,420	3,632	7,168	11,262	11,428
Whites	23,890	145,758	339,399	678,698	977,154	1,338,710

Bureau of the Census, Negro Population 1790-1915 (DC, G.P.O. 1918)

---

chapter 9

"Warfare and Strife" in Illinois

"We love this country and its liberties, if we could share an equal right in them."

Illinois also had a long history of tolerating slaveholders. In 1712, when France claimed the area, it legalized and encouraged the slave trade there. In 1720, Phillip Renault purchased enslaved Indian and African people in Santo Domingo to work as miners in Illinois. In 1770 a small section of southern Illinois on the border with Kentucky had thirty African and sixty Indian slaves.[1]

As a free man of color, Jean Baptiste Pointe Du Sable established a trading post under the British in 1779 that became the city of Chicago. In the next decade or two, after the United States assumed control from Britain, Illinois began to attract people with sharply contrasting views about bondage. In 1786, after the Northwest Ordinance opened the region, the Reverend James Lemon, a white Virginian, migrated to New Design, Illinois, and organized eight antislavery Baptist churches and founded the Anti-Slavery League. When other residents of the territory sent proslavery petitions to Congress, Lemon's Baptists countered with antislavery messages, and Lemon was chosen as a delegate to Illinois's first constitutional convention. By 1818, when Illinois entered the Union, fifty agents of his Illinois Anti-Slavery League were active throughout the state.

Virginia and Kentucky planters also flocked to the fresh soil of Illinois when their intensive labor and farming methods wore out their local soil. If slavery was to survive, it had to march westward and find new land. Slaves soon labored in the salt mines of Shawneetown, Illinois, on the Ohio River's border with Kentucky. Others were driven to mine lead in Galena, near the Mississippi River on Illinois's northwestern boundary with Iowa and Wisconsin.

Planters were delighted to find that in geography, soil, climate, and crops the Wabash Valley and southern Illinois had much in common with northern Virginia and Kentucky. Virginia and southern Illinois shared a geography and rainfall that produced good crops of corn, wheat, tobacco, and hemp. In fact, Cairo, Illinois, was farther south than Richmond, Virginia. Until the 1830s the views of slaveholders dominated southern Illinois and greatly influenced politics all over the state.[2]

In 1809, when Illinois separated from the Indiana Territory, its territorial legislature passed an indenture law similar to Indiana's. Indiana repealed its indenture law the next year, but Illinois continued to allow slaves to be held as indentured servants, and this dictated state policy into the first decade of statehood.

By 1813 legislation prohibited free people of color from entering the state and required Black residents to register with a court. The following year legislators authorized the use of slave labor in the Shawneetown saltworks, and by the 1820s Kentucky slaves laboring in the saltworks had made it "the largest industrial enterprise in the entire West."

As a result of indentured servant laws, in 1815, on a promise of four hundred dollars, a woman named Silvey signed an indenture to John Morris for forty years, and in 1818 one named Linda bound herself for ninety-nine years for the same amount. It is probable that both women were actually slaves and doubtful whether either one received the cash.[3]

In 1818 Illinois became a state, and within a year it also passed Black Laws borrowed from its territorial past. Its indenture laws meant that, again in defiance of the Northwest Ordinance, Illinois was another state to enter the Union with a form of legalized slavery.

In 1836 in *Boon v. Juliet*, Bennington Boon claimed indenture rights to Juliet's three children, though her indenture had legally expired. With aid from whites Juliet sued for her children's freedom, and a court declared her children free under Illinois law. In spite of this, the struggle against indenture proceeded slowly. In the 1840s, 350 African Americans were still held against their will in Indiana and Illinois, mainly in counties that bordered the Ohio River. Not until 1845 did the Illinois Supreme Court rule that holding indentured apprentices was a form of illegal bondage.[4]

For many African Americans in Illinois, the bondage imposed by indenture, the restrictions of the Black Laws, and bigoted officials proved overwhelming obstacles to happiness. In 1818, Abraham Camp, a leader among Black pioneers who lived in the Wabash River valley, wrote his judgment:

> I am a free man of colour, have a family and large connection of free people of colour residing on the Wabash, who are willing to leave America whenever the way shall be opened. We love this country and its liberties, if we could share an equal right in them; but our freedom is partial, and we have no hope that it ever will be otherwise here; therefore we had rather be gone, and though we should suffer hunger and nakedness for years.[5]

Statehood continued to bring further discriminatory provisions. In 1819 the Illinois legislature enacted a law imposing a $1.50-a-day fine on anyone who hired an African American not registered with the state. In 1829 the bond required of Black migrants was raised from $500 to $1,000.

By 1822 Illinois voters had elected a proslavery lieutenant governor and a controlling majority in both houses of the legislature. Statehood emboldened these politicians, and during the next two years they argued slavery would bring prosperity to Illinois and pursued an agenda that sharply divided the state.

In 1823 the proslavery legislature recommended a constitutional convention to legally restore bondage to Illinois. Their chief foe was Edward Coles, the recently elected governor, who had been born to a Virginia planter family. In 1819 he freed his slaves, purchased land for them in the West, and helped them become free farmers.

Though Coles won office by a narrow margin, he was ready to risk his political career to rid Illinois of its slavery laws. For eighteen months, Governor Coles rallied the opposition to the convention. He charged slave labor would bring economic ruin to the state and enshrine social injustice. Former governor Reynolds described the intense conflict that engulfed his fellow citizens.

> The convention question gave rise to two years of the most furious and boisterous excitement and contest that ever was visited on Illinois. Men, women and children entered the arena of party warfare and strife, and the families and neighborhoods were so divided and furious with bitter augment against one another, that is seemed a regular civil war might be the result.[6]

Clashes between supporters of the two factions, wrote Judge Gillespie, "for fierceness and rancor excelled anything ever before witnessed. The people were at the point of going to war with each other."

Another participant reported:

> Old friendships were sundered, families divided and neighborhoods arrayed in opposition to each other. Threats of personal violence were frequent, and personal collisions a frequent occurrence. As in times of warfare, every man expected an attack, and was prepared to meet it.

Finally, Illinois's white citizens trooped to the polls and, by a narrow 6,800-to-4,900 vote, rejected a proslavery convention. The idea of legalizing slavery disappeared, but so had Governor Coles's political future. In 1830 the Illinois census still listed 746 indentured servants, and three court rulings upheld the forced-labor system, one as late as 1843.[7]

Once Illinois entered the Union, African American resistance began to take more organized forms. From 1818 to 1822, as the

U.S. Congress met to consider bills to strengthen the Fugitive Slave Act of 1793, people of color in Illinois secretly mobilized to hide and help escapees. Benjamin Henderson, who purchased his own liberty, organized a secret station that relied on conductors of both races.

White antislavery figures began to play a more public role. From Jacksonville, west of Springfield, the Reverend Pat Henderson published *The Statesman*, perhaps the first antislavery newspaper west of the Allegheny Mountains. A German immigrant, the miller F. Grau, used his mill on the stagecoach route to Chicago to help people flee their chains.[8]

Despite threats of jail, fines, and personal dangers, in 1842 members of the Illinois Antislavery Society publicly swore they would never stop aiding fugitives and would never testify against anyone who did. The society asked citizens "to extend the hand of kindness and hospitality in *all things necessary for his escape,* to every panting fugitive from the Southern Prison House, who may come within the reach of their benevolence."

In 1843 this society announced that "to aid the slave catcher in the free States is no better than to aid the kidnapper on the coast of Africa." That same year the Putnam County society insisted fugitives were "peculiarly entitled to the sympathy of advice, assistance and comfort of the abolitionists; the penal laws of the State of Illinois notwithstanding."

Abolitionists found their work its own reward. In 1846 a white Chicago abolitionist revealed how he and his comrades helped thirteen escapees and looked forward to aiding many more during the winter. Chicago's mayor had called a meeting, he said, but antislavery people took it over, passed resolutions, and sang abolitionist songs. He rejoiced in the excitement: "We are having glorious times here or have had for the last ten days, from the attempt to return two Fugitive Slaves."[9]

Perhaps no figure in early Illinois history represented antislavery commitment more than a white minister named Elijah Lovejoy. He published his *Observer* in St. Louis until a proslavery mob destroyed his presses. In May 1836 he settled in Alton, Illinois, and by September his *Observer* was again rolling off the presses. In five months its circulation jumped

from a thousand to seventeen hundred copies.

Then, in August 1837, a white mob destroyed Lovejoy's press, and later, when another press arrived, they returned to throw it in the river. Meetings denounced the minister, but he remained defiant. "I dare not flee away from Alton," he said; "the contest has commenced here, and here it must be finished. . . . If I fall, my grave shall be made in Alton."

In November, when another mob assembled, Lovejoy, gun in hand, his younger brother, Owen, at his side, made his stand. The mob set the *Observer*'s building on fire, destroyed the press, and killed Elijah Lovejoy. A grand jury failed to indict any members of the mob.[10]

Lovejoy became the country's first notable antislavery martyr. The death of an editor defending his press meant the struggle against slavery had become part of a crusade to save American civil liberties. Many in Illinois blamed abolitionists for the trouble. A year after Lovejoy's death, the Illinois General Assembly adopted resolutions condemning abolitionist societies and urging a proslavery constitutional amendment. A young legislator named Abraham Lincoln was among the few to vote against both.

During this violent time, antislavery societies led by women in Illinois began to grow. Around 1842 the Putnam County Female Antislavery Society announced, "Slavery is the great crying sin of our country; it is the greatest moral and political evil that afflicts our nation and blots its fair fame. . . . Then should it not claim our first attention?"

Despite discriminatory laws, African American pioneers tried to advance. In 1831 William de Fleurville, a penniless Haitian barber, settled in New Salem, Illinois, where Abraham Lincoln introduced him to a local tavern so he could earn money as a barber. Fleurville settled in Springfield, married Phoebe Roundtree, and opened his shop opposite the town post office, the town's first barbering establishment.

He also advertised his talents in verse:

> *I scrapes the chin with hand so light,*
> *That to be shav'd is mere delight:*
> *And then I cuts the hair so well,*
> *That which is best you cannot tell.*[11]

Fleurville played clarinet and donated money to the Catholic church his family attended and to Protestant congregations. He became a popular local figure and, with Lincoln as his attorney, made some lucrative real estate investments. When he died in 1868, a local editor said his "funeral was one of the largest ever held in Springfield."

Thomas Jefferson Hunn, fleeing a harsh slave life in Kentucky, also reached Springfield. He changed his name to Houston and became an Underground Railroad conductor. He entered Kentucky, liberated his brother, and then helped him to rescue his wife and children. During the Civil War Houston served in the Union army, and afterward his family produced a host of attorneys, educators, and physicians—including the famous Charles H. Houston, who, at Howard University Law School, trained future Supreme Court justice Thurgood Marshall.[12]

* * *

John and Mary Richardson Jones of Chicago

The African American population of Illinois was 5,436 in 1850 and increased to 7,628 by 1860. By this time, most new-comers had settled far north of the Kentucky border. In 1833, Chicago, at Du Sable's post on Lake Michigan, was planned, and within two years it became a leading landing point for European immigrants. Many arrived carrying their belongings in "sacks on their shoulders," wrote an editor. In 1836, 450 ships arrived in Chicago's harbor and carpenters' hammers were heard throughout the town.

Finally incorporated in 1837, Chicago soon became a destination for runaways heading to Canada. Women members of the African Methodist Episcopal Quinn Chapel, still standing on 2401 South Wabash Avenue, hid and sped people on their way. A plaque at Beverly Avenue commemorates the Gardner home, which became "a refuge for slaves during the Civil War."

In 1845 a husband and wife, John Jones and Mary Richardson Jones, arrived in Chicago from the South with $3.50 and high hopes. John Jones was born free in North Carolina in 1816 to a light-skinned free woman and a German American named Bromfield. Fearing he might be enslaved, his mother apprenticed her son to a man who bound him to a Memphis, Tennessee, tailor. John, at twenty-two, returned to North Carolina where a judge ordered him released from his obligations and issued him "freedom papers."

Jones returned to Memphis, where he rekindled a relationship with Mary Richardson, the attractive daughter of a free blacksmith. In 1841 the couple moved to Alton, Illinois, and were married. For the next four years the Joneses took part in many of the town's legal and illegal antislavery activities.[13]

In 1844, John Jones asked the county clerk to affirm his free status in writing. The curious document said Jones was "entitled to be respected . . . in the due prosecution of his Lawful concerns." The clerk declared him "a resident or citizen of the State of Illinois."

Though little is known of Mary Richardson Jones's life, she

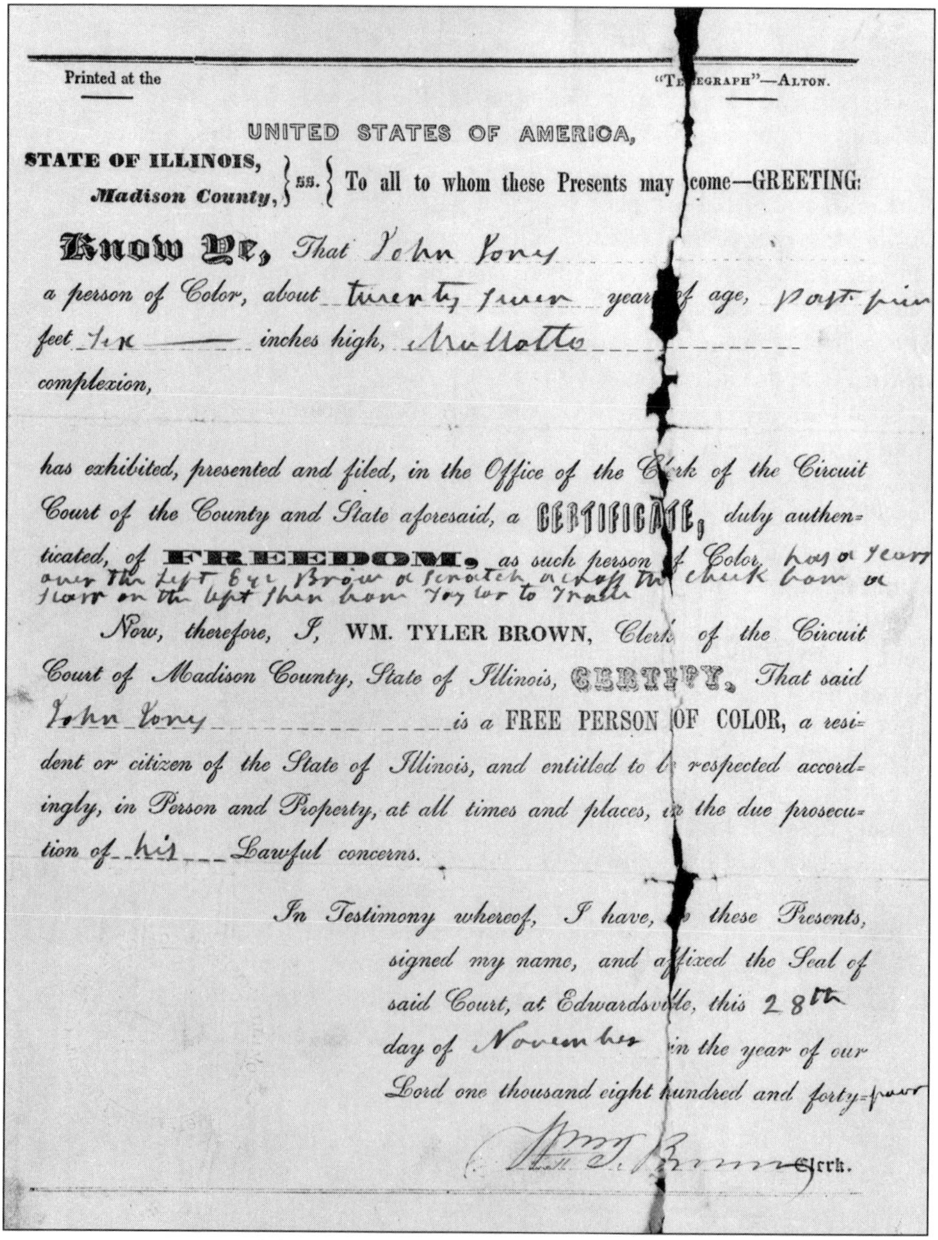

Printed at the "TELEGRAPH"—ALTON.

UNITED STATES OF AMERICA,

STATE OF ILLINOIS,
Madison County, } ss. { To all to whom these Presents may come—GREETING:

Know Ye, That *John Jony*
a person of Color, about *twenty seven* years of age, *post five*
feet *six* inches high, *Mullatto*
complexion,

has exhibited, presented and filed, in the Office of the Clerk of the Circuit
Court of the County and State aforesaid, a CERTIFICATE, duly authen-
ticated, of FREEDOM, as such person of Color *has a scarr*
over the left eye brow a scratch across the cheek bow a
scarr on the left thin bow Toyler to Trate

Now, therefore, I, WM. TYLER BROWN, Clerk of the Circuit
Court of Madison County, State of Illinois, CERTIFY, That said
John Jony is a FREE PERSON OF COLOR, a resi-
dent or citizen of the State of Illinois, and entitled to be respected accord-
ingly, in Person and Property, at all times and places, in the due prosecution of *his* Lawful concerns.

In Testimony whereof, I have, to these Presents,
signed my name, and affixed the Seal of
said Court, at Edwardsville, this 28th
day of *November* in the year of our
Lord one thousand eight hundred and forty-*four*

Clerk.

The 1844 freedom certificate of John Jones
when he was twenty-seven years old
[Chicago Historical Society]

shared her husband's taste for activism. In Chicago, the couple rented a home at 119 Dearborn Street, and he set up a tailoring business. Someone gave the family a start with two dollars of food credit at a local grocery. John and Mary probably taught themselves to read and write. They had one daughter, Lavinia.

The tailoring business made the Jones family prosperous and provided a cover for their secret activities. They turned their home into a station on the Underground Railroad credited with aiding dozens of escapees to reach safety in Canada.

In 1853 Jones, as a highly respected antislavery voice, served as vice president of an African American national convention in Rochester. During visits to Chicago, Frederick Douglass stayed at the home of the man he called "my old friend." When they launched western antislavery tours together, Jones and Douglass challenged hotel managers' efforts to segregate them from other dining-room guests.

John Jones (1817–1879) was painted after the Civil War by Aaron E. Darling [Photo courtesy of Illinois Historical Society]

In 1854 John advertised in Douglass's paper that his business was expanding. He offered to find jobs for reliable houseworkers, cooks, and waitresses, and to lend money, rent houses, and collect rents.[14]

Seeing them as intertwined strands in his people's liberation, Jones spearheaded both abolitionist and civil rights campaigns. In 1853 he spoke out against a new legislative effort to prohibit African American migration to the state, as the legislature continued to weaken the legal status of African American people. In 1847 the new Illinois Constitution included a provision that kept free African Americans from entering the state. However, since the legislators failed to enact an enforcement measure, it had remained an empty law.

Jones and his fellow citizens, lacking the vote and other citizen rights, fought for justice as best they could. In 1852 their Chicago Literary and Debating Society passed resolutions call-

Mary Richardson Jones (1819–1910) was painted after the Civil War by artist Aaron E. Darling. [Photo courtesy of Illinois Historical Society]

ing for repeal of a law denying them the right to give court testimony against whites. Though activists collected three thousand white signatures on their petitions, nothing changed.

In the mid-1850s battles for justice heated up. In 1855 Jones played a leading role in a Springfield convention calling for repeal of the state's Black Laws. That year men in Galena, Illinois, formed "the Order of Twelve" or "the Knights of Tabor," a secret African American society committed to liberation. Its members drilled with arms and planned "to do battle for the freedom of the bondsman." The society plotted a military strike at Atlanta, Georgia, in July 1857, but it was postponed because of a gathering storm.

Shortly after the Order of Twelve organized, Jones and fellow Chicagoan Allan Pinkerton, who was to be the director of President Lincoln's secret service during the Civil War, worked together on secret, illegal antislavery projects. Then, in 1856, Frederick Douglass brought abolitionist John Brown to the Jones home and the family heard his plan.[15]

The Joneses contributed to Brown's scheme, but after his first visit, John and Mary Jones, in particular, had doubts about his goal. Mary wrote this recollection:

> The first time I ever met John Brown he came to our house one afternoon with Fred Douglass. Mr. Douglass said he was a nice man. . . . I told Mr. Brown I thought he was a little off on the slavery question, and that I did not believe he could ever do what he wanted to do. The next morning I asked him if he had any family. He said: "Yes, madam, I have quite a large family, besides over a million other people I am looking out for, and some of these days I am

going to free them." I thought to myself, How are you going to free them?

Well, then, after that he dropped into our house most any time. He would talk about the slavery question and say what might be done in the hills and mountains of Pennsylvania; and Mr. Jones would say: "Why, Mr. Brown, that is all wind, and besides, you would lose your life if you undertook to carry out your plans." And I remember how Mr. Brown looked when he snapped his finger and said: "What do I care for my life—if I can free those Negroes?"

After being in Kansas awhile, he came on here with thirteen slaves. . . . I had been reading about how many men he had around him and I said to my husband: "I do not want John Brown's fighters. I am willing to take care of him, but not his fighters," but he said: "They are here, and I am going to let them in." Four or five of the roughest looking men I ever saw [entered]. They . . . looked like they were ready to fight, but they behaved very nicely.[16]

Mary Davenport arrived in Chicago in 1863 when she was seven years old. [Chicago Historical Society]

In 1860, when Chicago's black population had risen to 955, John Jones was leader of the Repeal Association, which accelerated the drive against discriminatory laws. As a twenty-five-year resident "paying taxes on thirty thousand dollars" but without "political status in your State," he appealed directly to Governor Richard Yates. Then, in 1864, Jones wrote and published a sixteen-page booklet, *The Black Laws of Illinois and a Few Reasons Why They Should Be Repealed.*

Jones's Repeal Association collected eleven thousand signatures on petitions and he brought them to the capital at Springfield, saying, "We have been treated as strangers in the land of our birth. Give us protection and treat us as you treat other citizens of the state. We ask only even handed justice." The next month, January 1865, near the end of the Civil War, Illinois Black Laws were repealed.

John Jones led the successful campaign to have his state become the first in the Union to ratify the Thirteenth Amendment, which ended slavery, and later the Fourteenth and Fifteenth Amendments promising equal rights. But his work was not finished. In 1866, along with Frederick Douglass and George T. Downing, Jones led an African American delegation to a dramatic White House confrontation with President Andrew Johnson. They argued with the president over justice, equal rights, and the future of Black people. They failed to win their point, but they had proven the president was no friend of African Americans.

In 1871 Chicago's Great Fire destroyed some of the Jones family's staggering eighty-five-thousand-dollar fortune in real estate, but still left them wealthy citizens. In 1872, Jones was elected to the Cook County Board of Commissioners, the first man of color elected to office in the West. He used the board as a forum to denounce segregated schools, and finally succeeded in this cause in 1874. The next year, however, Jones's bid for re-election was defeated.

In 1875 the Jones family publicly and proudly celebrated thirty years of crusading for liberty and justice in Chicago. The *Chicago Tribune* praised John Jones's success in business and as an activist, and his many philanthropic endeavors. He died in 1879, leaving a net worth of fifty-five thousand dollars.[17]

ILLINOIS Territory 1809; State 1818

Population growth:

	1810	1820	1830	1840	1850	1860
Blacks	781	1,374	2,384	3,929	5,436	7,628
Whites	11,501	58,837	155,061	472,254	816,034	1,704,291

Bureau of the Census, Negro Population 1790-1915 (DC, G.P.O. 1918)

chapter 10

The "Order of the Men of Oppression"

*"It was fight and run—danger at every turn [in Detroit],
but that we calculated upon, and were prepared for."*

In 1701 a Frenchman, Antoine de la Mothe, sieur de Cadillac,
led the first Europeans into the straits of the Detroit River. Soon
after, Africans seized from the British colonies during the war
with Napoleon were living inside the tall wooden walls of Fort
Detroit.

The loyalty of Africans became an issue during the French
and Indian War. Chief Pontiac of the Ottawa united eighteen
Native American nations to drive off the British, and seized
one British fort after another, and then
laid siege to Fort Detroit for eight
months. A white settler reported Pontiac's troops killed whites but "were
saving and caressing all the Negroes
they take." He worried lest this might
"produce an insurrection."[1]

After the Northwest Ordinance
brought U.S. law to the region, enslaved
African men and women began to sue
for liberty in Michigan territorial courts.
In Detroit, Peter and Hannah Denison
had been promised liberty by their master's will. When they learned the will
freed them, but left their eight children
in bondage, the Denisons asked a judge
to set the children free, but in 1807 the
court ruled against them.

Ottawa chief Pontiac besieged Detroit in 1763.
One white resident claimed he killed whites
but "saved" African Americans.

As a child in 1807, Elizabeth Denison escaped from Detroit after her parents' lawsuit for freedom for their children failed. She returned to Detroit, worked hard, and upon her death in 1866 left $1,500 to her church. [Photo courtesy of the Burton Collection, Detroit Public Library]

At this point, two of the children, Elizabeth and her brother Scipio, probably encouraged by their parents and aided by white friends, escaped to Canada. Elizabeth later returned to Detroit and in the 1820s served as a domestic with a white family. By 1825 she owned forty-eight acres of land in Pontiac, Michigan.

In 1827, the year Detroit was incorporated as a city, Elizabeth Denison was married in its Saint Paul's Protestant Episcopal Church. Her husband died several years later, and she continued to work as a servant. Through her savings, she bought stock in a steamboat, the *Michigan*, and a local bank.

Detroit grew rapidly. In 1831 lake steamers deposited immigrants at its docks and a local paper reported: "Almost every building that can be made to answer for a shelter is occupied and filled." By 1834, what had once been a tiny frontier village housed almost 5,000 white and 138 African American people, a theater, a museum, schools, churches, a library, a lyceum, a historical society, and a ladies' seminary. It boasted a water system, a sewage system, and streetlights that did not always work.

In 1837, the year Michigan entered the Union, Elizabeth Denison bought a lot in Detroit and began to pay off her mortgage. In 1854 she owned a home at the edge of the city's business district, and the next year she was able to travel to Paris. When she died in 1866, Denison's will bequeathed $1,500 to the Protestant Episcopal church so that "the rich and poor should meet together."[2]

Many people of both races who first arrived in Detroit later departed for southern Michigan or points west. Recently completed roads made travel easier. In 1832 a road to Chicago was

Early roads made travel slow and sometimes dangerous in frontier Michigan.

opened, and two years later a Territorial Road sent pioneers through rolling hills and level plains to St. Joseph, Michigan.[3]

Dawson Pompey, born a slave in Virginia in 1801, was freed by his father-master and sent to Ohio. He arrived with enough money to start a career training and trading racehorses. In the 1830s Pompey married a white woman and they settled in Couvert, Michigan, where he was the first resident of color. The couple, with their growing family of eventually ten children, attracted other families of both races to their community. In the 1850s the couple watched their children rise in local economic and political life. Seven of Pompey's sons served in the Union army.[4]

Like most frontier families, Ruth and Thornton Blackburn wanted to live, work, and prosper in peace, and they began life in Michigan that way. In July 1831 the Blackburns escaped from slavery in Kentucky to settle and take jobs in Detroit. Everyone seemed to admire the couple's honesty, hard work, and frontier grit. The *Detroit Courier* praised Thornton Blackburn as "a respectable, honest and industrious man."

Then in early June 1833, a Kentucky posse rode in and had the Blackburns arrested. Detroit's African American community shifted to battle alert. People packed a Saturday court session, where the couple refused to deny they had been slaves. When rumors spread that the Blackburns could not get a fair hearing, Black men loaded their weapons and women began to discuss a less violent course of action.

Tempers rose in the city when the Kentuckians demanded the Blackburns. Sheriff John Wilson rejected the request and kept them in his custody. By Sunday, the many friends and allies of the Blackburns had devised some complicated tactics to rescue the couple. Men began to deploy near the jail with clubs and guns.

That Sunday Black women put into operation their own plan, one that did not rely on ugly weapons. A delegation of African American women visited Mrs. Ruth Blackburn in her cell. Mrs. George French secretly exchanged clothes with Mrs. Blackburn, who then walked out with the delegation. That night Ruth Blackburn was secreted to Canada. When authorities released

Mrs. French, she also left for Canada. Detroit's Black women had scored an impressive nonviolent victory.

On Monday crowds of muttering African American men armed with stones, clubs, and pistols milled around the jail. Since white stereotypes cast men of color as weak, fearful, and unassertive, no one paid attention. A Detroit paper said the men at the jail were engaged in impulsive or silly posturing, not to be taken seriously.

Later that day Sheriff Wilson decided to order to the jail a horse and cart that would carry Thornton Blackburn to the wharf, where a steamboat would return him to Kentucky. When the prisoner appeared, a seething mob swung into action. Some placed Blackburn on the cart and rode off. When Sheriff Wilson tried to disperse the crowd, he was beaten to the ground, his skull fractured, and some teeth knocked out.

As the sheriff's cart carried Blackburn away, a posse raced in pursuit. It only found the empty wagon. By nightfall, Thornton and Ruth Blackburn were reunited in Canada.

Mayor Marshall Chapin declared an insurrection and summoned federal troops, and Company E of the Fourth U.S. Artillery Regiment arrived to guard Detroit. City officials arrested about thirty African Americans for aiding a fugitive and assaulting a lawman, but no one was convicted. Later the sheriff died of the injuries he suffered in what was called "the Blackburn riots."

In Canada the Blackburns were briefly arrested and then released. By 1852 Thornton Blackburn had become a vice president of the Canadian Mill and Mercantile Company in Buxton, Canada West, and in 1870 a Canadian paper reported that he was a wealthy citizen of Toronto.[5]

Though Michigan entered the Union in 1837 as a free state, its legislature soon passed a set of restrictive Black Laws. To even enter Michigan, an African American had to produce a court certificate of freedom and to post a five-hundred-dollar bond pledging good behavior.

White antislavery societies, which had started during Michi-

Michigan reformer Laura S. Haviland, photographed displaying some of slavery's chains, which she helped to break.

gan's territorial days, began to challenge the Black Laws. In 1832, Elizabeth Chandler and Laura Smith Haviland, young white Quakers, formed the Logan Female Anti-Slavery Society. This was the first women's organization created in Michigan and the Northwest Territory.

For Haviland, this was the start of a long, dedicated, and perilous fight against racial injustice. Soon she and her husband founded the Raisin Institute to educate people of every race. Laura Haviland also became a conductor in Michigan's Underground Railroad.

Haviland described her commitment in these words:

Let a slaveholder come and try us. . . . Let them . . . disturb an escaped slave, at any time of the night or day, and the sound of a tin horn would be heard, with a dozen more answering it in different directions, and men enough would gather around the trembling fugitive for his rescue. For *women* can blow horns, and *men* can run.

Even when a slaveholder arrived with witnesses and reams of legal documents, she wrote, "it would avail him nothing, as we claim a higher law than wicked enactments."

Though her life was threatened and her work took her far from home and family, Haviland's zeal never flagged. Her husband died, and so did her first son, but her dedication to others never died. Though Tennessee offered three thousand dollars for her capture, she often entered slave states to guide women, men, and children to Canada. She particularly tried to rescue women fugitives targeted by posses seeking high rewards.[6]

In 1852, when Calvin Fairbanks, a courageous white conductor, was thrown into a Louisville, Kentucky, cell, Haviland's response to the "suffering brother in jail" was immediate. Louisville papers threatened to arrest her, but Haviland visited Fairbanks carrying fresh clothes and some cash.

Haviland was only one of Michigan's daring activists of both races who defied posses to lead runaways to Canada. One Underground Railroad network began in the southwest corner of the state and moved through Cassopolis, Schoolcraft, Climax, Battle Creek, Marshall, Albion, and Jackson. In these and other locations close to the Michigan Central Railroad tracks, conductors saw that men, women, and children reached the Detroit River's crossing into Canada.

In the 1840s two fugitive cases demonstrated the heroism of ordinary frontier people. In 1846 the Crosswhites or Crosswaits, learning family members were about to be sold, fled Kentucky with their four children. With a posse in pursuit, the family separated and then reunited in Marshall, Michigan, where they bought a house on East Mansion Street.

The Crosswhites arranged with neighbors who agreed to fire a shot should a posse ride in. On an early, cold January morning in 1847 three Kentuckians tried to shoot their way into the Crosswhite home but the family had bolted the door. The shots, said a white friend, "had the effect of rousing the neighborhood. . . . An old gentleman mounted on his horse, rode through the streets ringing a bell, crying 'Kidnappers—the Crosswait family,' until the whole town was gathered about the house of the fugitives." Black and white friends helped the Crosswhites reach Detroit and Canada.[7]

In 1849, other Michigan Quakers effectively stopped a slave-hunting posse. Five members of an enslaved family from Kentucky fled to Quakers in Young's Prairie, where many Black families lived. The African Americans, a white neighbor reported, "owned small patches of ground on which they had erected comfortable little log houses, and by their industry and thrift managed to live very comfortably."

When scouts from Kentucky discovered the colony, thirty slaveholders and posse men arrived, some with wagons to carry back all the Black people they intended to seize. Posses rode into Niles and fanned out for simultaneous raids on isolated homes in the countryside.

Slave catchers pushed into one cabin and seized a mother and three sons. In another, a wife escaped through the window and gave the alarm to a white man, who rode for help. Another white raced after a writ of habeas corpus that would prevent Black people from being carried off by the posse. "There were desperate struggles at many of the cabins, and a number of fugitives were bruised and wounded, before they were overpowered," Levi Coffin later reported.

By daylight a force of two hundred irate citizens raced after the Kentuckians. When they finally confronted them, the posse men pulled out revolvers and bowie knives. But a white blacksmith named Bill Jones led his men, knocking the Kentuckians about with fence posts. After Quakers stepped in to prevent serious injuries, the cowed posse were glad to leave their prisoners and ride home. Prisoners embraced their rescuers and then fled to Canada.[8]

Lambert, DeBaptiste, and "the African American Mysteries"

By the 1840s a full-scale Black migration to Michigan was under way. The state's African American population tripled each decade, rising in 1850 to 2,583, with 600 living in Detroit. With help from people like Laura Haviland, these pioneers began to find their American dream in Detroit.

The daring and commitment of two recently arrived Black men and their families also insured that Detroit was a safe port for fugitives. Long before they met in Detroit, William Lambert and George DeBaptiste had led similar lives. Both were born free around 1815, became barbers at an early age, and married. Their families arrived in Detroit eight years apart, the Lamberts in 1838 and the DeBaptistes in 1846.[9]

Lambert was born in Trenton, New Jersey, to a father who

had purchased his freedom and a mother who had been born free. He was educated by Quakers and held jobs as a cook, a shoemaker, a barber, and a tailor. In 1838, at twenty-three, he settled in Detroit. Two years later he addressed a city meeting to demand the vote for his people, and was drawn into the Black protest movement. He joined a Vigilant Committee that served as a watchdog and voice for his community.

By this time African Americans in Detroit had generated a host of cultural activities, including a debating club, a library, a reading room, a young men's group, and more than a dozen self-improvement societies. As a father of two sons, Lambert began to organize a day school in a church. He gained public attention when a white newspaper called him "a young Negro of unmixed blood" whose political writing was marked by "good sense and good taste."

Lambert and other young reformers tried to mobilize people behind campaigns for Black education, self-help, and antislavery. These young people advocated education for all children and adults, opposed the use of liquor, and called on the community to utilize its many cultural institutions.

In 1843 Lambert wrote the announcement call for Michigan's first African American protest convention and served as its temporary chairman. He urged delegates to "organize, organize, organize" for an "unceasing war against the high-handed wrongs of the hideous monster Tyranny." African Americans, he told the twenty-three delegates, were "determined to be free," and he demanded they promote "Education, Temperance, Industry, and Morality." Delegates made a strong denunciation of slavery and Black Laws.[10]

Lambert went on to help establish Saint Matthew's Protestant Episcopal Church and served throughout his life as its warden and a lay leader. He sought forums to denounce the city's caste system, its denial of education to all children, and its refusal to open decent jobs to his people.

George DeBaptiste was born to free parents in Fredericksburg, Virginia. Since it was illegal for even free people of color to learn to read and write in the state, he taught himself in secret. After working as a servant for wealthy whites, he settled in

William Lambert after the Civil War

Indiana and began a trading business on the Ohio River. A certificate he carried to Indiana in 1835 described him as a "mulatto boy" twenty years old and five foot seven inches in height.

To assist runaways, DeBaptiste allowed male fugitives to use his certificate thirty-three times. After he was arrested for his rescue efforts, a Madison court convicted him of failing to post a bond when he entered Indiana, and he was ordered deported. With attorney Stephen C. Stevens, a former justice of the Indiana Supreme Court, he convinced an appeals court to nullify the order. The court ruled expulsion would place DeBaptiste in the hands of slaveholders "contrary to morality and religion."[11]

General William Henry Harrison, who had been territorial governor of Indiana, hired DeBaptiste as his personal servant. In 1840, when Harrison became president of the United States, DeBaptiste served as his steward at the White House. Then, a month after inauguration, Harrison died and DeBaptiste returned to Madison, Indiana. He opened a barbershop and continued to aid fugitives, reporting that in eight years he helped 108 men, women, and children reach safety.

In 1846 DeBaptiste and his family moved to Detroit, hired a teacher, and opened their home as a classroom for Black children. Soon after, he met Lambert, and the two men began to enroll others in a hard-hitting, armed antislavery unit called the African American Mysteries.

DeBaptiste was, in the words of one scholar, a "bold, ingenious man, courageous, thoroughly devoted to his cause." Not since the Blackburn rescue had Detroit witnessed so large, sophisticated, and daring a rescue organization as the African American Mysteries. Sometimes their rescue society was also called the Order of the Men of Oppression. It was manned by fearless and dedicated members.

The African American Mysteries did not have long to wait. Robert Cromwell, seized in Detroit by a slave-hunting posse, pleaded for help. Lambert and DeBaptiste led their troops into his courthouse, seized Cromwell, and spirited him to Canada. Then Lambert hired a white attorney, who had the posse men arrested. "Our law point was bad," Lambert later admitted, "but we were many in number and resolute."

In the decades before the Civil War and with Canada only a river away, Detroit attracted many escapees. Though both men, as successful entrepreneurs, risked a great deal, they managed to keep the African American Mysteries busy. DeBaptiste served as its manager, and Lambert as its secretary. Said Lambert: "The general plan was freedom."

The Order of the Men of Oppression carried titles ranging from "ruler" to "black knight" to "knight of Saint Domingo." To qualify, members had to study major slave revolts and revolutions, and how governments worked, and had to memorize elaborate signals and rituals. The Grand Lodge, or headquarters, was on Jefferson Avenue between Bates and Randolph Streets, and fugitives were led in at night from Ann Arbor and Wayne.[12]

Years later Lambert recalled harrowing nights when sheriffs or slave-hunting posses tried to uncover their secret operations. "It was fight and run—danger at every turn," he said, "but that we calculated upon, and were prepared for."

Earlier, when Lambert and DeBaptiste found that Detroit's white abolitionists rarely invited people of color to their meetings, they questioned their intentions and goodwill. The two then decided the Order of the Men of Oppression would be controlled and largely staffed by people of color. Lambert described how members

> arranged passwords and grips and a ritual, but we were always suspicious of the white man, and so those admitted were always put to severe tests, and we had one ritual for them alone and a chapter to test them in. To the privileges of the rest of the order they were not admitted.[13]

However, the Order of the Men of Oppression did admit Richard Realf, a white. And years later Lambert recalled the time when he found in abolitionist John Brown a white man he fully trusted. Brown entered the Grand Lodge with twenty to thirty fugitives, and according to Lambert they became "firmest friends." In 1858 the two met again when Brown summoned associates to discuss his plan for an assault on Harpers Ferry.

Despite the demands of the African American Mysteries, Lambert and DeBaptiste found time to continue their businesses. DeBaptiste had an interest in a barbershop, became chief clerk in a clothing store, and bought a bakery. Selling the bakery, he bought a steamship, the *T. Whitney,* that ran between Detroit and Sandusky. Later he sold the steamship and used the cash to finance a catering business.

DeBaptiste and Lambert continued their antislavery labors through the Civil War. DeBaptiste toured Michigan during the war to recruit an African American regiment and spent six months in South Carolina training his recruits.

After the war DeBaptiste was a leading city caterer and president of the Negro Union League, which he helped finance. He mobilized his community to send school supplies to education-hungry former slaves in the south.

In April 1870, William Lambert, thin and sporting a slight beard, chaired the celebration for passage of the Fifteenth Amendment to the Constitution, granting Black men the vote. George DeBaptiste, joking about past dangers, also took part. Toussaint L'Ouverture, Lambert's oldest son, read President Grant's proclamation on the amendment to a crowd that included Michigan governor Henry Baldwin, police officers, former abolitionist allies of both colors, and local officials.

A few months later George DeBaptiste became the first Black elected delegate to the state Republican nominating convention. For the next four decades African American men in Michigan followed in his footsteps to city, county, and state Republican conventions.

The two directors of the African American Mysteries had become Michigan's wealthiest African Americans. When DeBaptiste died in 1875 a white newspaper praised him as "a firm friend of his race" and "an active energetic man, very genial, wholesouled, generous, and an agreeable social companion." Lambert, also energetic, genial, and a friend of his people, died in 1890 leaving a seventy-thousand-dollar fortune.

In the decade before the Civil War, and despite the efforts of the Lamberts, DeBaptistes, and others, Michigan had increased restrictions on people of color. In an 1850 referendum, its white males voted 32,026 to 12,840 against opening elections to people of color. However, the results proved that even at the height of the slave era more than a fourth of Michigan voters approved of Black participation in state government.[15]

In 1863 Black men from Michigan, finally welcomed into the Union army, helped defeat the Confederacy and end slavery. Michigan, though a solidly Republican state, did not move as swiftly toward racial equality.

In 1867 Michigan's ninety-nine Republican legislators were committed to equal rights and its thirty-three Democratic legislators were strongly opposed. But when a new constitution with equal voting rights appeared on the ballot, the Democrats played on white fears and ratification was defeated 110,582 to 71,733 votes with only five of Michigan's fifty-nine counties in favor. Now 40 percent of white voters had asked that Black citizens be allowed to play an equal role in government.

In 1870 the electorate finally approved male African American suffrage 54,105 to 50,598 votes. This narrow victory followed ratification by the states of three amendments to the U.S. Constitution that ended slavery and promised equality, including voting rights.[16]

Michigan's white males, having strongly rejected Black voting rights before and after the Civil War, now barely approved it, even after passage of three major constitutional amendments promising equality. Black pioneers, despite bold efforts to win their rights, faced new uphill battles.

MICHIGAN Territory 1805; State 1837

Population growth:

	1810	1820	1830	1840	1850	1860
Blacks	144	174	293	707	2,583	6,799
Whites	4,618	8,722	31,346	21,500	395,071	736,142

Bureau of the Census, Negro Population 1790-1915 (DC, G.P.O. 1918)

---

chapter 11

The Iowa of Alexander Clark

"They came at night and were . . . glad to camp on the floor."

In the last quarter of the seventeenth century, French explorers passed through Iowa and claimed it as part of what would become the Louisiana Territory. This entire territory, from New Orleans in the south to Iowa, Minnesota, and Montana's border with the Rocky Mountains in the north, was purchased from France in 1803 by the United States. Until the 1830s the northern Mississippi Valley was largely inhabited by Native Americans. The Sioux and Chippewa controlled northern Minnesota, the Sauk and Fox ruled the upper Mississippi south of them, the Iowa dominated the Des Moines River that bisected Iowa, and the Oto, Missouri, and Omaha nations governed the Missouri Valley that swept north and westward from St. Louis. During the early decades of the nineteenth century, pioneers had to gain permission from an Indian nation to settle. Iowa had failed to attract settlers for other reasons, too. It was mainly covered with grass taller than the wheels of prairie schooners, and its soil was considered too hard to farm.

Finally, in 1832, the United States defeated Chief Black Hawk and his Sauk and Fox followers. Within a year the federal government, heeding the pleas of land-hungry settlers living in the adjacent states of Indiana, Illinois, Kentucky, and Missouri, opened Iowa for settlement. Settlement remained slow in the 1830s, as homesteaders on the east side of the Mississippi struggled with their crops, and Iowa farmers were still engaged in major Indian wars. Iowa was part of the Michigan Territory until 1836, when it was added to the Wisconsin Territory, and two years later it was transformed into an independent Iowa Territory.

Iowa entered the Union in 1846, but six years later Native Americans still stubbornly refused to surrender their land to the newcomers. Fort Des Moines remained more a fort than a town, and its city charter was still five years away.

However, the word had spread eastward that in the Fox language Iowa meant "this is the land," and this increasingly attracted newcomers. Six years before statehood Iowa had forty-three thousand white settlers, and many "squatter" families who lacked a legal right to their land. These squatters mobilized into "Claim Associations" to fight outside land speculators who bought large tracts of land to hold empty until land prices increased.[1]

Probably the earliest people of African descent to set down roots in Iowa were fleeing slaves from Missouri who were welcomed into Native American villages. An 1832 report on runaways in Iowa found they "were usually warmly received and often intermarried with the Indians." One Black man, John, enslaved by an Indian trader near Des Moines, was able to hire out his own time. In 1838 "Mogawk," described as a tall, dark man, lived among Poweshiek Indians on the Iowa River.

During Iowa's territorial era, some African American pioneers also were welcomed into white communities. In 1834, six years before Dubuque was incorporated as a town, its Methodists opened Iowa's first church. Six African Americans, including two women, were among the charter members and, according to Methodist records, donated from twelve to fifty cents to their church.[2]

During territorial days African American fugitives from Missouri learned to trust the Quakers who lived in the counties bordering Missouri. Statehood was still six years away when the Quakers of Salem village and elsewhere reached out to fugitives, and thus established the first stations of the Underground Railroad in Iowa. Other religious farmers in two other counties not far from Missouri also hid runaways, helping them elude their pursuers and find liberty.

In 1838 the Iowa Territory banned slavery, but its 1840 census listed 188 African Americans, including 6 enslaved males and 10 enslaved females. Most of these were servants, such as the woman Stephen W. Kearney brought in 1834, and two other women who cooked for construction workers at the Sauk and Fox Indian agency.[3]

By 1842 white women in Henry County had organized a Female Antislavery Society. Drusilla Unthank spoke for its members when she said, "[A]s intelligent and accountable beings, it is our duty thus to act . . . [on] subjects of vital importance to the welfare of our country."

Though Iowa was the first state west of the Mississippi River to enter the Union as a slave-free state, its leading political figures treated ownership of slaves not as illegal or immoral but as bestowing high status. In 1837 George W. Jones, the territory's first congressman, was also Dubuque's largest slaveholder. In 1841, territorial governor John Chambers arrived from Kentucky with his slaves. Territorial secretary O. H. Stull came from Maryland bringing seven or eight men and women who were, wrote

In 1841 Iowa's first territorial governor, John Chambers, brought his slaves from Kentucky. He and other high Iowa officials saw ownership of human beings as a status symbol, as they had in the South.

an eyewitness, "kept in profound ignorance of the fact that when they touched the soil of Iowa they were free."[4]

Iowa's free air soon had the enslaved challenging its officials. In 1843, when Governor Chambers's term ended, a man and a woman he had held demanded and won their freedom.

In their struggle for justice some African Americans found staunch white allies in Iowa. In 1839, Ralph, enslaved in Missouri, had been sent by his owner to work in Dubuque. One day he was seized by two Virginia slave hunters who had plans to sell him. A leading city attorney rose to Ralph's defense, and Judge Thomas A. Wilson issued a habeas corpus order that stopped the two from holding Ralph. In court Ralph's lawyer proved he was not a runaway but had an owner in Missouri for whom he earned money.

The attorney argued that the Missouri Compromise, which drew a line banning slavery north of Missouri, automatically made Iowa free territory. This, argued the attorney, entitled Ralph to live as a free man, and Judge Wilson agreed. In Iowa his decision stood as a landmark victory for human liberty. A year later a grateful Ralph walked up to Judge Wilson and asked to work, as he said, "one day every spring to show you that I never forget you."[5]

Other white residents of the territory also followed their conscience on the issue of slavery. In 1839 J. H. Armstrong, who in Ohio in the 1830s was an Underground Railroad conductor, moved to a home on the Missouri border. He opened a secret station and conducted fugitives along a route that passed northwest through Denmark and Salem. In 1852, after Armstrong moved to a new home only four miles from the Missouri line, he started another, even busier station.

Though slavery had few supporters in Iowa, legislators feared that free African Americans might overrun their land. In 1838 the territorial legislature required that any person of color planning to enter the state had to show a certificate of freedom and post a five-hundred-dollar bond. Two years later the legislature banned interracial marriages.

In 1844, when the state constitutional convention met, fewer than a hundred African Americans lived in Iowa's more than fifty-six thousand square miles. Fearful delegates representing thirty thousand whites voted to impose harsh Black Laws on African Americans, and many wanted to turn away all Black migrants. One delegate warned ominously that a Black presence could lead to racial "amalgamation." Another said he would "never consent to open the doors of our beautiful state" to people of African descent.[6]

That same year, however, armed white Iowans rode out to defend nine runaway men, women, and children who chose Iowa

as their haven. The nine had been pursued by a Missouri posse who then convinced local officials to arrest them. When the nine struggled to escape, nearby whites rushed to their aid. In the confusion abolitionists spirited two away to liberty, and a woman, a child, and a man escaped on their own. Four runaways were caught and marched back to Missouri.

The next year, when an interracial couple settled in Marion County, white "amalgamation" fears returned. In 1845 Thomas and Rose Ann McGregor of Illinois staked a claim and began to farm. Some white neighbors were upset that a white man had married an attractive, spirited woman of color. Officials indicted the couple for violating the ban on intermarriage. The McGregors were able to have the court venue changed to Oskaloosa, where there was a large Quaker population. There a grand jury quashed the charge.

But the Marion County commissioners were not finished.

Slave hunters rode into Iowa, only to find Black and white resistance to their kidnapping efforts.

They ordered Mrs. McGregor to produce free papers and post a bond of five hundred dollars by January 1846 or "be sold to the highest bidder." When the couple defied the order, the sheriff and his deputy were sent to their farm to arrest Rose Ann McGregor on a day her husband was away. Ever resourceful, she barred the door, refused to listen to their arguments, and let them know she was armed and a crack shot. When night came, the lawmen shattered her door and seized Mrs. McGregor before she could fire her muzzle-loader.

The irate woman was bound and mounted on the deputy's horse for the ride to Knoxville. But about a mile from her home Mrs. McGregor dug her heels into the horse and it bolted into the night, leaving the startled lawmen behind. The next day Mr. and Mrs. McGregor appeared at the Marion courthouse and posted a bond. But after a few months they pulled up stakes to seek a more hospitable home.[7]

By the time of the Civil War, "Chloe" was among those African Americans who had settled in Iowa and other states of the Old Northwest.

By statehood, some of Iowa's African American population had begun to achieve economic success. In 1840, in Muscatine, a Mississippi River town near Iowa's southeastern corner, twenty-five black settlers constituted 5 percent of the town's population, and by 1850 their numbers doubled. A few did very well. Thomas Motts arrived in 1837 and soon operated his own

barber shop, and by 1850 he owned real estate valued at six thousand dollars, making him the most prosperous African American in town.

In 1848 four African American men organized Muscatine's AME church, the first in the state. By the following summer congregants had conducted a highly successful August First fair attended by the "fashionable ladies of the town." In Muscatine the AME Church held August First festivities each year, and soon white citizens began to appear as speakers.

By 1850 the African American community in Muscatine proudly sent all of its eighteen children to an elementary school taught by an

African American woman from Kentucky.

As in territorial days, whites, often Quakers, in Iowa continued to aid fleeing slaves. In Salem, Henry County, Henderson Lewelling, a white Quaker, lived in a stone house with a tunnel beneath it. He hid runaways in the tunnel and defied slave hunters. In Keosauqua, on the Missouri border, the Pearson house, built in the 1840s, had two cellars used to hide fugitives from Missouri.[8]

By 1854 Fayette County in northeast Iowa was home for the Basses, a large, intrepid Black pioneer family. In the 1830s Quaker aid had helped Sion Bass and his wife leave Virginia for Indiana. In the 1840s eighty Bass members moved to Illinois only to find hostile white neighbors. Less than half of their children had the opportunity to learn to read, and only four of twenty-four children were allowed to attend school. The Basses then built a school associated with their church, and it became the center of community life.

From Illinois, Bass sons led half of the original family, including more than a dozen school-age children, to Iowa. When they first appeared in Fayette, whites were antagonistic, and the community decided to keep to itself. With the Reverend George

A picnic in early Washington, Iowa, date unknown. [Nebraska Historical Society]

Watrous as their minister, the settlement soon brought in successful crops, and built schools, and people made friends.[9]

Missouri slaves continued to seek refuge in southern Iowa. Pursued by a posse, Ruel Daggs led eight Missouri slaves to Salem, where his Quaker friends refused to surrender any of them and forced the posse to leave. A few days later, when a heavily armed Missouri band arrived to confront the Quakers, they discovered the eight had already fled northward.

In the 1850s Charlotta Pyles opened her Keokuk home to fleeing Missouri fugitives. White abolitionists supported her efforts as she launched a tour of eastern states to raise money to purchase her relatives still in bondage.

By the time fiery John Brown arrived in Iowa in the 1850s with his plans for launching an antislavery war in Virginia, he found ready allies and supporters among whites and African Americans. Isaac Brandt of Des Moines recalled meeting Brown in early 1859 as he guided fugitives to Canada. They spoke few words and relied on hand signals developed for their secret work. Brandt said:

> It was a winter day, but I was out in the yard when I saw a covered wagon drawn along the rough road with a man walking at the side whom I recognized at once. He halted at my place and I called him to the gate. I saw that he had a load in his wagon and gave him the signal for safety and he understood. I asked him how many, and he held up four fingers of his hand. It was early in the day and he went on eastward with his "fodder" as we would have said. But in a few words exchanged he showed his passionate earnestness in the cause to which he had dedicated his life.
>
> I went to the wagon and peeked under the hay and cornstalks and saw four negroes keeping very quiet as they journeyed to they knew not where.[10]

Iowan John Todd, also an ardent supporter of Brown, was a white former Oberlin College student who turned his home and barn into an Underground Railroad station. In 1854 and 1856 Brown used Todd's home in Tabor, near the Missouri border, as a headquarters. Today the Todd home has a historical marker.

In 1853, in Lewis, the Reverend George B. Hitchcock, a white Congregationalist circuit rider, built a sandstone home he used as a church, an inn for travelers, and a hiding place for runaways. In Denmark, white Congregational minister Theron Trowbridge served as a conductor. On May 27, 1857, as the struggle over slavery heated up, the *Madison Plain Dealer* denounced him for "negro-stealing" while "professing the religion of the gospel." It suggested hanging as a punishment.

In Des Moines, Josiah Grinnell operated a leading station at Cherry Place. Grinnell was an abolitionist, a friend of John Brown, and a pioneer Iowan of many accomplishments. He founded the town of Grinnell, planned Grinnell College, helped launch the state's Republican Party, and served in Congress during the Civil War.

He left this description of the winter of 1859, when Brown hid fugitives in Grinnell's "liberty room."

John Brown's antislavery labors took him to Grinnell, Iowa, as he led fugitives to Canada.

> They came at night and were the darkest, saddest specimens of humanity I have ever seen, glad to camp on the floor, with the veteran as a night guard, with his dog and miniature arsenal ready for use on the alarm.[11]

Alexander H. Clark

Alexander H. Clark, one of Iowa's leading African American voices for freedom, was born in 1826 in Pennsylvania to former slaves. At age thirteen he moved to Cincinnati and lived with an uncle who taught him barbering. He briefly attended school and at fifteen he took a job on the Ohio steamer *George Washington* as a bartender.

The next year the teenager got off at Muscatine, purchased a house, married, began to raise a family, and stayed for the next forty-two years. At one time his real estate investments totaled $1,200 and made him the second wealthiest African American in town.

Clark devoted his considerable oratorical skills, talent, and money to advance his community's interests. In 1849 he and three other men founded the AME church in Muscatine. That year he was chosen to be the speaker at his community's August First emancipation celebration. He went on to play a leading role in black Masonic lodges. When Clark was sued for hiding Jim, a runaway, his argument in his own defense won a judicial decision that ended all forms of bondage in Iowa.

In 1857, Clark initiated a petition campaign to repeal Iowa's Black Laws, and gathered 122 white and Black signatures. The same month Clark was among the thirty-three delegates who gathered in Muscatine's African Methodist Episcopal church for the state's first Black convention. They demanded full citizenship and agreed that education was the path to "the moral and political elevation of the colored race."[12]

That same year white Iowans called a new constitutional convention with Black suffrage the main issue. Though twenty-one of the thirty-six delegates were Republicans, the convention majority rejected an equal voting rights bill, and instead asked voters to decide the matter. At a moment when fewer than three hundred Black people lived in the state, white voters turned down equal suffrage 49,511 to 8,489, or about six to one.

However, Clark and other community leaders took heart when President Lincoln began his cautious steps toward emancipation during the Civil War. In 1862, Clark asked Governor Samuel J. Kirkwood to let him raise a company of Black volunteers, only to be told it was "a white man's war." Emancipation changed everything a year later. At Keokuk, Clark was allowed to recruit 1,153 African Americans into the First Iowa Volunteers—and was chosen as the regiment's sergeant major. Though he failed the physical exam because of a leg injury, his proudest moment came when he presented the regimental banner, sewn by the African American women of Keokuk, to the regiment he had recruited.[13]

In one major battle Black Iowans faced Jo Shelby's Confederate raiders, who outnumbered them three to one. "During the whole fight the colored men stood up to their duty like veterans," wrote their white commander. He had nothing but praise for his men's "strong arms and cool heads, backed by fearless daring." He concluded: "Never did men, under such circumstances, show greater pluck or daring."

After the war, Clark's reputation rose among all Iowans and his civil rights activities increased. In 1868 he spoke to the thirty delegates at an African American convention at the capital in Des Moines. To white Iowans, he read the convention's address, which called for equal rights in the name of Iowa's five hundred Black Civil War volunteers, and the Declaration of Independence.

That year Clark sued Muscatine's school board for refusing to admit his daughter, Susan, to a public school. With state attorney general O'Connor serving as his lawyer, he appealed to the Iowa Supreme Court, and it outlawed school segregation. His daughter graduated high school in 1871.[14]

In 1869 Clark served as a vice president of the Iowa Republican convention, and four years later as a delegate to the Republican National Convention. In 1873 President Grant wanted to appoint him consul to Haiti, but he declined the position. In 1876 he represented Iowa at the mammoth U.S. Centennial Exposition in Philadelphia.

In 1880 Clark, then fifty-four, attended the Republican state convention and spoke on behalf of Iowa's African American delegates. Clark's son became the first African American to graduate from the University of Iowa Law School and Clark became the second. As an attorney, he divided his time between his legal office in Muscatine and editing his newspaper, the *Chicago Conservator.*

Through his paper and public speeches, Clark protested the failure of the federal government to deliver the equality promised his people during the Civil War and by the three amendments to the Constitution that followed. He died in 1891 while serving as a special U.S. envoy in Liberia.[15]

IOWA Territory 1838; State 1846

Population growth:

	1850	1860
Blacks	188	333
Whites	42,924	191,881

Bureau of the Census, Negro Population 1790-1915 (DC, G.P.O. 1918)

---

chapter 12

Wisconsin Battles "The Heel of Oppression"

"Free men to the rescue!"

In 1824, more than two decades before Wisconsin became a state, an African American woman headed there seeking freedom. Light-skinned Caroline Quarelles, sixteen, fled St. Louis, Missouri, after her owner cut off her long black hair. A $300 reward was posted for her capture and a posse rode after her. Quarelles took a steamboat to Alton, Illinois, and then boarded

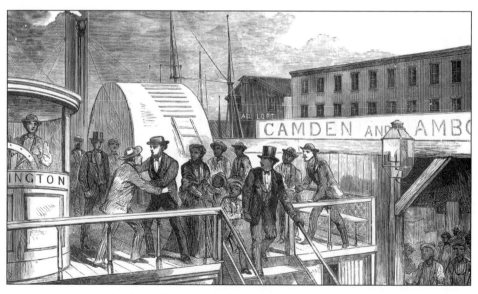

Caroline Quarelles was not the only runaway to flee bondage by steamboat. Here Abolitionists rescued Jane Johnson and her children from slavery.

a stagecoach for Milwaukee, Wisconsin. From there Underground Railroad conductors guided her westward to Waukesha, and then on to Detroit, where she crossed into Windsor, Canada. The young woman's dramatic escape reveals that many whites in what was to become the Wisconsin Territory were prepared to defy the law to aid fugitives.[1]

Few other African Americans found any reason to venture into this land north of Illinois, though frontier trapper Jim Beckwourth traveled through at least once. In 1836 the Wisconsin Territory was organized, and four years later, as Illinois's overflow population moved northward, census takers found 30,749 whites and 196 people of color living on its plains.

Many early Wisconsin settlers, including German immigrants, were opposed to slavery's extension to the west, and some were outright abolitionists. Five years after it entered the Union, in 1853, a crowded meeting in the state listened carefully as a runaway described the evils of the southern bondage from which he had escaped. The audience included one white man who believed that "much good will be done by this injured son of Africa and that he will be a means in God's hands, of assisting in the overthrow of the diabolical sin of American Slavery."[2]

Underground Railroad stations began to appear along Wisconsin's southern border. In Janesville the twenty-room brick Tallman House was built by its owners to hold fugitives in the attic and basement, and with a lookout on the roof. A bell was rung when escapees approached, and servants standing at a stained-glass window waved them in. The cellar door was also left open. At night people were led from the house to the Rock River, where conductors ferried them northward to Milton.

In March 1854, white residents in Racine, Wisconsin, became incensed when U.S. marshals seized Joshua Glover, an African American neighbor, under the new Fugitive Slave Law. Hearing that Glover had been beaten, thrown in a wagon, and driven to jail in Milwaukee, citizens of Racine convened at the town's largest meeting until that time. Many marched to the courthouse square to demand that the unjust law be repealed.

Then a hundred of them made the boat trip to Milwaukee to

ensure that Glover received a fair trial. They found five thousand equally enraged Milwaukeeans had formed their own Committee of Vigilance to see that justice was done in Glover's hearing before a judge.

Sherman Booth, editor of the *Daily Free Democrat*, took command of the antislavery crowd and rode through the streets shouting, "Free men to the rescue! Slave catchers in our midst!" When officials summoned the local militia to control angry protestors, its members failed to appear. Soon excited, unruly crowds gathered at the jail to demand Glover's release. Angry men finally lost patience, battered in the door, took Glover, and put him in a wagon bound for Canada.[3]

For his role, Booth was tried and jailed. But he continued to write editorials charging that the federal government acted like a slave catcher. He warned readers that federal officials aimed "to establish the law of Slavery and kidnapping on the free soil of Wisconsin."

The Booth controversy stirred citizens. The state supreme court freed Booth in a decision that virtually declared the 1850 Federal Fugitive Slave Law unconstitutional. When the editor was jailed again, another mob freed him. As his federal case dragged on, his supporters raised one thousand dollars for his fine. But Booth refused to pay the fine and elected to stay in prison, suggesting the money go to his wife. From jail he announced: "I think I am doing more here than I could out." He even refused a presidential pardon.

Booth's case wound its way up to Supreme Court chief justice Roger Taney, no friend of Black justice. He ruled that Booth should be jailed for thirty days and fined a thousand dollars. Two days before Lincoln's inauguration, Booth, highly popular in the North, was pardoned and released by orders of President Buchanan.[4]

Their experience with Glover and Booth helped shape the white attitude in Wisconsin toward their Black neighbors. In 1848 Wisconsin entered the Union without restrictions on African Americans migrants, the only western state without any Black laws.[5]

The new constitution empowered the legislature to grant people of color voting rights if the white electorate approved this in a special election. In 1849 most voters chose to stay home for the referendum and it passed by a narrow 1,190 votes. However, officials called the result invalid because the votes cast amounted to a minority of the more than 31,000 who voted in the regular election. African Americans were determined to reverse the ruling.

Wisconsin's white citizens, including many who had supported Booth, proved less than enthusiastic about granting African Americans voting rights. In 1857 Wisconsin again debated allowing Black men to vote. This time, although citizens picked a Republican governor, they rejected Black suffrage 40,106 to 27,550. Democrats were quick to point out that the new Republican Party's legislators also had failed to support the issue.

That same year Wisconsin's African American leaders, who referred to the denial of their right to vote as "the heel of oppression," strongly petitioned for an end to "taxation without representation." Their petition insisted they be granted the same rights as new immigrants to the United States. African Americans continued to call protest meetings demanding the vote. The white opposition to equal voting began to lose ground

Black people, such as the man next to the prairie schooner, crossed into the Old Northwest with pioneer wagon trains. [Minnesota Historical Society]

as a majority of Republicans shifted to support suffrage.

Meanwhile, newly arrived African American pioneers built sturdy communities in the state. In 1849 fugitive slaves seeking liberty and their own land founded Pleasant Ridge in western Wisconsin. Six years later Walter Stewart founded the town of Forest. In 1855 Wesley Barton settled in western Wisconsin, and four years later was appointed postmaster of Barton Corners, now Burr Corners.[6]

In 1845 Moses and Catherine Stanton founded Stantonville, which became a station on the Underground Railroad. Mrs. Stanton, who had been a princess of the Narraganset Indian nation, had six children, and the family also adopted a nephew. During the Civil War William Stanton joined Company I of the Wisconsin Volunteer Infantry. Stantonville was later renamed Chilton.[7]

In 1857, as Racine's African American population grew, some formed the St. Paul Missionary Baptist Church, the first Black church in the state. In these early years Kenosha boasted four Underground Railroad stations, three run by white ministers.[8]

By 1860 the Black population of the new state had grown to more than a thousand, a fivefold increase in twenty years. Whites, however, increased twentyfold during the same period.

Many more African Americans reached Wisconsin during the turbulence of the Civil War years. At sixteen Ansel Clark had twice been sold by his southern owners and forced to serve in the Confederate army. Liberated by General William Tecumseh Sherman's Union army, he fled northward on the Underground Railroad. After a job as a chef on a Great Lakes steamer, Clark settled in Portage, where he bought a comfortable two-story home on West Wisconsin Street and became a constable, a volunteer fireman, and a humane society official.[9]

August Cohen, another slave liberated by Sherman's army, settled in Kenosha. Peter D. Thomas, also a slave who served in the Civil War, settled in Racine and became the county's first African American elected to office. John Miles, another Black Civil War veteran from Wisconsin, found his final resting place in Milwaukee's Forest Home Cemetery.

In 1865 Wisconsin's African American population was larger

and more determined than before. They pointed to their battle-field bravery against the Confederacy and stated that they were taxed and liable for military duty as other citizens. Their petition asked the legislature for equal suffrage.

The next year, 1866, seventeen years after the first vote that denied African Americans suffrage, Wisconsin's supreme court issued an odd ruling. It now ruled the equal rights referendum of 1849 had really passed, and had been the law in Wisconsin all along.

Despite this ruling, the struggle for equal rights was far from over. In 1870 former slaves living in the village of Pleasant Ridge initiated the state's first integrated school district.

Black citizens of Wisconsin still faced discrimination. In September 1889 Owen Howell, an African American, sent a white messenger to purchase his ticket for *The Runaway Wife* at Milwaukee's Bijou Opera House. When Howell appeared to take his seat, an usher refused to seat him and tried to send him to the gallery. Howell left the theater not to comply but to hire an attorney.

The rector of St. Paul's Episcopal Church accused the theater of "contemptible barbarism," and other prominent whites rushed to Howell's defense. At a Black convention, delegates listed discrimination at "certain hotels, restaurants, barber shops, public inns and places of amusement" as well as life insurance companies and state jobs. They called for

Black Laws in the North and West continued to segregate whites from African Americans in the 1850s. A Black passenger is asked to leave a white section of a train.

political action, organized a Civil Rights League, and endorsed a white senator they could trust. Governor William D. Hoard supported their initiatives, and prominent whites and African Americans accused "poorly-educated" whites of bigotry.

Judge Daniel H. Johnson heard the *Howell v. Lit* case in a

courtroom filled with people of color. "In this case you must find for the plaintiff," he told the jury, and they awarded Howell $152 in damages and costs. Though a Democrat, Johnson ruled the Constitution had "made unlawful every discrimination on account of color or race." In Wisconsin, he said, "no separate schools are provided" because "all men are equal in law."[10]

The next year Black Milwaukee citizens drafted and introduced to the legislature an antidiscrimination bill, and two African American men testified on its behalf. It did not pass until 1895, and then only after African American leaders mobilized their community to reward their friends and punish enemies on election days.

WISCONSIN Territory 1836; State 1848

Population growth:

	1840	1850	1860
Blacks	196	635	1,171
Whites	30,749	304,756	773,693

Bureau of the Census, Negro Population 1790-1915 (DC, G.P.O. 1918)

---

chapter 13

The Greys of Minnesota

*"There has not been a moment in my life when I regretted
that my feet had touched the soil of Minnesota."*

Minnesota, from its birth as a territory in 1849 with four thousand settlers to its statehood nine years later, failed to attract
many African Americans. Though by 1860 the state population
stood at over six thousand whites and only thirty-nine Blacks,
people of color had made their contribution to the state for
decades.

Long before it became a U.S. territory, African Americans
took part in the fur trade in Minnesota. They served in the profession's three main occupations: managing business affairs and
supervising trading stores; serv-
ing as voyageurs, whose canoes
carried pelts eastward and returned with goods to barter;
and as hunters, who worked
alongside Indians searching for
game.[1]

Among Minnesota's early
Black pathfinders were James P.
Beckwourth and John Brazo,
both of whom entered the upper
Missouri River and worked for
the American Fur Company.
Brazo was described as "hardy
and courageous" and a "full-
blood Aethiopian" who spoke

*Black
frontiersman
Jim
Beckwourth
traveled
through early
Wisconsin and
Minnesota as a
fur trader.*

French, English, and several Indian languages. Beckwourth was a tough frontiersman, army scout, and adventurer whose journeys took him from St. Louis westward to California and south to Florida during half a century of wilderness life.

The best known of Minnesota's Black trappers were descendants of Jean Bonga and his wife, an enslaved couple who arrived in the late 1700s and settled near Leech Lake in the north. Around 1800 their son Pierre accompanied his owner, Canadian trader Alexander Henry, on Northwest Company trapping expeditions to the Red River. Henry often left Bonga and a white man in charge of various company forts.

Pierre married a woman from the neighboring Chippewa nation, and their son, George, was born a few years later. In 1872, late in life, George Bonga wrote: "I was born somewhere near where Duluth now is . . . pretty near 70 years ago." His father was able to see that George "when . . . a little boy . . . went to school in Montreal." He learned to speak French, English and various Indian languages.

Stephen Bonga, of the noted fur-trapping family, was photographed in Superior City, Wisconsin, by W. D. Baldwin. [Minnesota Historical Society]

Like his father, young George worked for the Canadian Hudson's Bay Company, which took over the Northwest Company, and also married a Chippewa woman. While still a teenager, in 1820, he served as an interpreter with the Chippewa for Michigan territorial governor Lewis Cass. In 1837, at Fort Snelling, near today's Minneapolis, he negotiated an important treaty for Cass with the Chippewa. In 1848 Cass became a presidential candidate.

George Bonga, known for his deep ebony color and his great strength, was able to carry as much as seven hundred pounds of furs and goods, and once carried this amount over the portage trails of The Dalles of the St. Louis River in northeastern Minnesota. He also once risked his life to track an accused murderer through Sioux land, then captured him and hauled him back for a trial at Fort Snelling.

George Bonga and his wife maintained homes

at Lac Platte, Otter Tail Lake, and Leech Lake, and he later became an independent trader. In 1857, Benjamin Densmore, a railroad surveyor and a visitor to the Bonga home, reported being greeted by "a gruff voice, replete with good naturedness . . . a hearty handshake" and a warm meal. During dinner Bonga not only proved an entertaining host but revealed his knowledge of elections and political matters in general. Bungo Township in northern Minnesota is named for this trapping family.[2]

Perhaps the best-known African American man to touch Minnesota soil was the slave Dred Scott. In 1836 Scott and his owner reached Fort Snelling, where Dred married Harriet Robinson in a ceremony performed by an Indian agent. For two years the Scott family lived among the fort's 150 civilians, and one of their two children was born there.

Because Minnesota was free land, Harriet and her husband later decided to sue for their liberty and that of their two daughters. The famous *Dred Scott* case took more than ten years to finally reach the U.S. Supreme Court, which then struck down their appeal for liberty. However, within months a new master had freed Harriet and Dred Scott.[3]

Harriet Robinson and Dred Scott met and were married at Fort Snelling by an Indian agent. For eleven years they fought the U.S. legal system to win freedom for their two daughters and themselves.

Fort Snelling, near St. Paul, where Dred Scott married Harriet Robinson, and where the couple lived for two years.

* * *

Perhaps due to their small numbers, life for people of color in early Minnesota was bounded by few restrictions. In the 1830s Minnesotans attended a school of thirty pupils, and the teacher's diary spoke of children of "English, French, Swiss, Swedish . . . Indian, and Negro extraction." Pupils may have included the children of James Thompson, who in 1827 met and married a Sioux woman at Fort Snelling.

In the 1830s a missionary had purchased Thompson for $1,500 to serve as his Indian interpreter. Later, Thompson moved to a cluster of small huts that would not be called St. Paul until 1846. In the next decade Thompson's money, lumber, and shingles helped build a Methodist church on Market Street. In 1871 James Thompson was probably the first of his race invited to attend an Old Settlers' Association meeting.[4]

More than a few enslaved people in Minnesota sought liberty through the territorial judicial system. Between 1831 and 1834, an enslaved woman named Rachael, brought by her master to several army posts, became one of the first Black people to sue for freedom in the West. Though her plea reached the territorial supreme court, the court refused to free her.[5]

Six years before statehood, the *Minnesota Pioneer* described the three dozen people of color in the region, saying they were "attentive to their business . . . and here, on the confines of barbarism, do as much to put a civilized aspect on the face of society as any other class." Even so, two years later white legislators introduced a bill requiring Blacks who wished to enter the land to post a $500 bond. It was defeated.

Jane Grey Swisshelm, one of the first U.S. women to edit a newspaper, used her *St. Cloud Visitor* to denounce southern masters who brought their slaves to Minnesota. When a proslavery mob destroyed her press, Swisshelm was the first woman to be attacked for using her freedom of the press.

In 1860 Colonel R. Christmas of Tennessee was on vacation with his family at Lake Harriet, a St. Anthony, Minnesota, resort. He brought his slave, Eliza Winston. Winston announced that Christmas had promised her liberty, only to change his mind. She finally got word to Emily Grey, a leader in the African American community. She said "she wanted to be free and was held against her will." Grey's antislavery friends saw that Winston's demand was heard by a judge.

In a courtroom surrounded by an unruly crowd demanding liberty and justice for the young woman, Judge Vanderburg heard her claims and declared her free because she had been brought to free territory.[6]

Since this decision contradicted the recent Supreme Court decision in the *Dred Scott* case, proslavery forces mobilized to seize Winston. At this point another judge, William Babbitt, took Winston to his house for protection. A mob prepared to storm his home, but the judge fired a shot that sent people racing home. Next, abolitionists, outnumbering their foes five to one, arrived to rescue the judge and Winston and send her on her way to safety in Canada.

Although Minnesota African American children often attended schools with whites in territorial days, this began to change with statehood. In 1858 Black parents in St. Paul became the first to have to demand that their children attend classes alongside whites. The board answered that if fifteen

Black pupils attended a school for three months, the city would pay costs, and a segregated school soon opened.

During the Civil War, school integration again became a state issue. In 1864, near Lake Como, a Sunday school principal enrolled two Black children in his class, but white parents demanded their expulsion. The *St. Paul Daily Press* scoffed at those "who profess to be white people . . . [but] have yet given another evidence of their inferiority and ignorance." The editor added his own view that Black children earlier had learned lessons alongside white children in St. Paul, and that state law mandated school integration. But it was not until 1868 that the legislature opened public schools to all pupils.

In 1865 Minnesotans also wrestled with the issue of equal voting. When the legislature voted for equal manhood suffrage, a voter referendum rejected it. Three years later, the *Minneapolis Tribune* denounced bigots who would reduce a Black man to "a serf in a country which he has shed his blood to save," and Black male suffrage won legislative approval. Minnesota's African American population began to rise sharply, doubling in ten years to 1,564 in 1870 and doubling again by 1880.[7]

The Greys of Early St. Paul

Emily Goodridge, born in 1834 to a former slave family in Pennsylvania, shared a love of frontier life with her sister, Mary, and three brothers. Mary and her brothers left to settle in Saginaw, Michigan, where the young men became photographers and Mary operated a hairdressing parlor.

In the 1850s, Emily married Ralph Grey, and they soon had

a daughter. Ralph left to start a business in a new town called Minneapolis, and in 1857, eighteen months later, now a successful barber, he summoned his family to join him.

Accompanied by her husband's cousin and his new bride, Emily Grey and her two-year-old child endured heavy, delaying rains, and "ham and eggs for breakfast, eggs and ham for dinner, and by way of variety, for supper we were given the same old dish—ham and eggs." Despite all, she recalled later "the best of humor prevailed."[8]

The foursome traveled first by steamboat; then, paying a dollar each, they boarded the Concord stagecoach heading to St. Anthony Falls. They enjoyed being treated like everyone else, finally reaching Minneapolis, "quite a small village, located on the west bank of the Mississippi and opposite the city of St. Anthony."

The Grey family first lived at the Jarrett House, where Ralph served as a barber. Emily Grey was tall, with a large frame, bluish gray eyes, a fair complexion, and freckles on her nose. Friends described her personality as "kind, understanding, polite, dynamic and determined."

Her family, she wrote in a fascinating diary, found little animosity in Minnesota. On the contrary,

Eula Ross Grey brought to light Emily Grey's diary many years later. [Minnesota Historical Society]

> every person we came in contact with seemed to be doing his utmost to make it pleasant as could be for

us. Civility and kindness seemed to be in the air in those good old pioneer days. You breathed it in with every inhalation of the atmosphere.

The couple built a home in an old barn, Emily recalled, "humble and unpretentious in appearance. . . . I papered it with my own hands alone one day, as a surprise to my husband when he came home that night." Husband and wife then "formed ourselves into an executive committee" to select and purchase provisions and furniture.[9]

The Greys expected to find very few neighbors of African descent. "Very soon after my arrival, I became acquainted with all the persons of color," Emily Grey wrote, listing sixteen names.

> When I met so many faces of colored men, women and children in my travels throughout the city, it seems marvelous, so like a dream, and the surprise is increased from the fact that I have learned that we are a [large] population of colored American citizens. . . .

Like many pioneer women, Emily at first bemoaned "the lack of women's companionship" and was pleased to find many other women in her neighborhood. "First one neighbor called and then another, until we became acquainted and our visiting relations were easy and smooth."[10]

Soon "good, old-time neighborly calls" surrounded the family with friendly people. "There was always some woman friend who would gladly be to me a guiding star to lead me out of the many difficulties met with all households."

The Reverend Charles Seccombe and his wife were among the Greys' first white visitors. The white minister offered a "Christianlike invitation to attend services at the [First] Congregational Church [of St. Anthony] of which he was pastor."

Emily Grey was delighted with her new life.

> I feel constrained to record the fact that there has not been a moment in my life when I regretted that my feet had touched the soil of Minnesota. . . . In the after years, you will consider the pioneer days as

among the happiest. Oh! The good neighborly fel-
lowship, you can never forget.[11]

Emily and Ralph Grey were accepted into the Minnesota Ter-
ritorial Pioneers, those settlers who arrived before statehood.
Known for his education, intelligence, and oratorical skills,
Ralph was chosen to read the Emancipation Proclamation at a
Black convention.

Emily participated in the St. Thomas
Episcopal Church Mission, the
women's exhibit at the 1893
Chicago World's Fair, and many
local social events. She had
four children, wrote her warm,
optimistic, charming memoirs
in 1893, and died in 1916. Her
daughter later adapted her
memoirs for publication.

In the Civil War, 104 men of
color volunteered to serve in
Minnesota out of a Black population of only 259, which included
women and children. This outstanding
contribution to the Union led the *St.
Paul Daily Pioneer* to state that "the
boasted superiority of the white race
over the Negro is so purely ficti-
tious, so purely the result of conven-
tional arrangements."[12]

The Reverend Robert Hickman, who organized a massive escape from Missouri that ended in St. Paul in 1863. [Minnesota Historical Society]

In north central Missouri, a young slave, Robert Hickman, organized dozens and dozens of other enslaved people, perhaps as
many as 200, in a bold strike for liberty. Calling themselves "pil-
grims," they built a raft near the Missouri River, and one night
boarded it. They headed eastward to the Mississippi and then
pushed northward into Minnesota and freedom.

The Hickman pilgrim saga comes down to us with several
variations. In one version the mass flight was aided by northern
soldiers, and in another their raft was towed by a Mississippi

steamer. What is clear is that these brave women and men reached St. Paul, where they formed the Pilgrim Baptist Church with Hickman as minister. Some of the young men joined the Union army, and others packed up for other parts of the West. In 1877 Hickman was formally ordained as a Baptist minister.[13]

MINNESOTA Territory 1849; State 1858

Population:

	1860
Blacks	39
Whites	6,038

Bureau of the Census, Negro Population 1790-1915 (DC, G.P.O. 1918)

chapter 14

From Missouri to Kansas:
The Odyssey of Henry Clay Bruce

"[I] would have sold my life very dearly had they over-taken us in our flight. How could I have done otherwise in the presence of the girl I loved."

Missouri and Kansas entered the Union two generations apart but formed explosive milestones on the march to the American Civil War. In 1819 Congress first argued endlessly, deadlocked, and finally agreed to the "Missouri Compromise." The issue at stake was whether slavery would be allowed in states that were carved out of the Louisiana Territory. The North and the South wanted to ensure their views on bondage prevailed as the nation marched westward.

To accept Missouri as a slave state would have upset the balance between eleven free and eleven slave states in the Union. To preserve the balance, Maine had been brought into the Union as a free state at the same time. To end their three months of wrangling, congressmen had also banned slavery, except in Missouri, north of the latitude line of 36 degrees and 30 minutes. The compromise did not satisfy either side. Slaveholders opposed any effort to confine slavery. They knew their labor system quickly wore out the soil and there was always a need to expand. Northerners resented opening new western lands to human bondage. Thomas Jefferson called the Missouri Compromise "a fire-bell in the night."

Jefferson's fire-bell continued to sound a warning. After the Mexican War, southern senators demanded that the new lands taken from Mexico in Utah and New Mexico be opened to slavery. The Compromise of 1850 tried to settle that issue. It

In the 1850s Kansas became a new escape route for runaways from Missouri. This picture is an antislavery attack on the 1850 Fugitive Slave Law. [Library of Congress]

Kansas governor Andrew Reeder donned a peddler's clothes to flee proslavery raiders.

allowed settlers in the areas to vote for slavery when states entered the Union. The compromise also included a strict Fugitive Slave Law that made a slave catcher out of the federal government and legally required people in free states to help posses capture runaways.

In 1854, the Kansas Territory, on the western border of Missouri, required another compromise. Senator Stephen Douglas proposed a "squatter sovereignty" compromise. It allowed Kansas settlers to decide the slavery issue. Douglas hoped to ride into the White House on its acceptance. But on election day in 1855, as residents prepared to vote slavery up or down, five thousand armed white Missourians swarmed into Kansas, seized polling booths, and cast four times as many ballots as there were voters in Kansas.

Raiders from Missouri turned Kansas into a battleground. When the governor objected to the Missouri ballot steal, he was dismissed from office and had to flee Kansas disguised as a peddler. "Every white-livered abolitionist who dared set foot in Kansas" was threatened with death, and an abolitionist was defined as "every man north of the

Mason-Dixon line." The New England Immigrant Aid Society made plans to send twenty thousand antislavery migrants into Kansas before the year was out. Northerners collected money to furnish the newcomers with rifles and ammunition.

In Kansas proslavery government legislators prepared for war by passing laws limiting free speech and free press for antislavery forces. They also made sure local officials met the needs of slaveholders.

Frederick Douglass proposed his Kansas solution. He would send "an army of one thousand" Black families "as a wall of living fire to guard it." From a base in Kansas, John Brown killed proslavery men and led forays into Missouri to liberate slaves and escort them triumphantly to Kansas and north. Out of the ashes of Kansas towns such as Lawrence, burned to the ground by Missouri raiders, came a Republican Party committed to halting slavery's expansion to the west.

Proslavery Missouri men cross into Kansas to vote in 1856.

When more than a hundred of his foes attacked and burned John Brown's camp at Osawatomie, the old abolitionist told his son Jason: "I will die fighting for this cause. There will be no more peace in this land until slavery is done for." Like Jefferson's, his words would prove prophetic.

Missouri

St. Louis was founded in 1763 by French adventurers from New Orleans. After the Louisiana Purchase in 1803, Americans arrived in St. Louis to find less than a thousand residents, and a fourth were enslaved Africans. Nearby Native Americans, unsubdued by these foreign intrusions, posed a threat to the town's safety.[1]

In 1804, when the Lewis and Clark expedition into the Louisiana Territory made its winter camp in St. Louis, Clark's slave, York, became the first of his race to appear by name in the chronicles of the town. He was a skilled hunter and fisherman and a formidable athlete, and he mastered new languages easily. York worked with Sacagawea, the young Shoshone woman who was the expedition's translator, and also proved valuable as an ambassador of goodwill to wary Native Americans.[2]

In 1810, St. Louis's 1,400 residents included 400 slaves and a few free people of color. The presence of hundreds of enslaved people at the edge of a wilderness still controlled by Native Americans made whites nervous. Masters found discipline hard to enforce, and African Americans sniffed the free western winds. A hiring-out system that allowed slaves to contract and receive wages for their work was profitable for the masters, but it also weakened the chains of bondage. Owners believed the main problem was lax supervision, which allowed enslaved people to carry extra cash and freely mix with whites and free people of color. For the enslaved, the city provided a taste of the forbidden fruit. Some African Americans learned to read and write, others purchased their freedom, and more than a few gathered their belongings and left for the wilderness.[3]

Slaveholders continued to arrive in St. Louis. Most brought only one or two slaves, and often both owner and slave headed into the wilderness. By 1820 the city counted 3,000 African Americans, about a third of the total of those in the Missouri Territory. Many were skilled crafts workers or domestic laborers.

Because most whites in St. Louis had few slaves, they did not require a special slave quarter. Instead, most African Americans worked alongside and lived in the homes of their masters or employers. This living arrangement further eroded the strict authority that would be enforced on plantations, and gave enslaved people opportunities to expand their horizons.[4]

St. Louis, as a fur-trading center and gateway to the frontier, continued to attract the adventurous. In 1817, five years before statehood, African American James Beckwourth, nineteen, an apprentice to a St. Louis blacksmith, felt the lure of the wilderness. When his boss tried to put a stop to his right to come and go as he pleased, he slugged the man and fled west for a life of adventure among Native Americans and fur traders.

In the 1850s, in northern Missouri, Polly Bruce, a slave, was determined that her son Henry and her other children would have the education she was denied. Since some planters did not prevent enslaved people from getting an education, Henry found he could buy a book anytime he "had the money to pay for it." But Missouri's free people of color, he wrote in his autobiography,

> . . . really had but few more privileges than the slave. They had to choose guardians to transact all their business, even to writing them a pass to go from one township to another in the same county. They could not own real estate in their own right, except through their guardian, neither could they sell their crop without his written consent.[5]

In March 1864, during the Civil War, Henry Bruce's young life reached a crisis when his master forbade him to marry another slave. The couple made their own plans. "She met me at the appointed time and place with her entire worldly effects tied up in a handkerchief, and I took her up on the horse behind me." With Bruce carrying a pair of Colt revolvers, the couple raced northward on country roads, a posse in pursuit. Bruce remembered being ready for any danger. He was

> . . . nerved for action and would have sold my life very dearly had they overtaken us in our flight. How could I have done otherwise in the presence of the girl I loved, one who had forsaken mother, sister and brothers and had placed herself entirely under my care and protection.

The couple traveled by train, ferried across the Missouri River, and landed in Fort Leavenworth, Kansas, with $5 and their clothes. They handed their cash to the Reverend John Turner of the AME church and that day he married them in his parlor. The next morning Henry Bruce met a brick contractor he had known in Missouri and was hired at $2.75 a day.[6]

Other fugitives found their way to Kansas during and after the war, but Bruce found that freedom had given them little else than the management of their personal lives.

Henry C. Bruce

They were set free without a dollar, without a foot of land, and without the wherewithal to get the next meal even, and this too by a great Christian nation, whose domain is dotted over with religious institutions and whose missionaries in heathen lands, are seeking to convert the heathen to belief in their Christian religion and their Christian morality.

In Leavenworth, Bruce and other African Americans found themselves in competition with Irish immigrants for the lowest-paid jobs. The fear the Irish had of losing their jobs often turned to rage. One Sunday night a mob of Irish laborers surrounded the Baptist church on Third and Kiowa Streets that Bruce attended. In the vacant lot behind the church, dozens of armed Irish and African Americans confronted each other. Curses and threats were exchanged, but bloodshed was avoided when the Irish decided to leave.[7]

John Berry Meachum

John Berry Meachum, born a slave in Virginia, was trained as a skilled carpenter, cooper, and cabinetmaker. He saved enough money to purchase his freedom, married, and soon after Missouri entered the Union in 1821, he followed his enslaved wife to St. Louis. There he prospered and used his savings to purchase his wife and children. Around 1826 he opened a barrel factory and ran it for the next ten years with twenty slaves he had purchased. In the factory, the slaves developed skills and then worked to pay for their freedom.[8]

Meachum was ordained as a Baptist minister and founded the First African Baptist Church of St. Louis, the first African

American Protestant church west of the Mississippi River. In 1847 Missouri law outlawed slave education, but even before then Meachum encouraged children and adults to learn all they could. He secretly taught people to read and write in Sunday school classes. To prevent authorities from uncovering his plan, he built a steamboat with a library inside and anchored it on the Mississippi River, where it was free of state rules. Each day pupils came aboard his floating school to learn how to read and write. Meachum died before the Civil War, but not before he had taught a generation of Black Missouri children, including future scholar and activist James Milton Turner.

By 1847, other schools for people of color operated in Missouri. From 1816 to 1826 in St. Charles, Timothy Flint, a white missionary, conducted one school. In the 1830s whites at Marion College taught African Americans, and in St. Louis some Catholics conducted classes for them.

In 1856 Hiram Revels, destined to become the first African American U.S. senator from Mississippi, opened his St. Louis school to 150 free people who were charged a dollar a month for each pupil. In Hannibal, Black Methodist minister Tom Henderson ran a similar school. During the Civil War it was taught by Blanche K. Bruce, brother of Henry Bruce, who later in Mississippi became the second African American to be elected to the United States Senate.[9]

Mississippi's two Black senators, B. K. Bruce and Hiram Revels, are portrayed on either side of Frederick Douglass.

During the Civil War the shackles of slavery began to melt in Missouri, a state that remained loyal to the Union. Each year it became increasingly easy to desert plantations for the Union army or the free states. In 1860, one hundred thousand people in Missouri were enslaved; some fifteen thousand of these had fled two years later, and by 1864 only twenty-two thousand were still in chains. In four years of war the price of a slave dropped from $1,300 to $100.

In St. Louis, the war and emancipation had persuaded citizens of both colors to open schools for African Americans. By 1865, a Black board of education managed four schools with four hundred pupils and eight teachers. That year, a Black high school opened with fifty students. White hostility to Black education remained high, and in 1863 a school for sixty pupils was open for only three days before it was burned down. Bigots often targeted the men and women who taught African Americans with threats, intimidation, and sometimes violence.[10]

Attorney James Milton Turner defended Black Cherokee claims in a U.S. court and won.

James Milton Turner

In 1840 James Milton Turner was born a slave in St. Louis County, Missouri, to John and Hannah Turner. In 1844, John was able to purchase his wife and son. Nuns at the St. Louis Catholic Cathedral conducted a secret school where young

Turner received his education. He next attended the Reverend John B. Meachum's school in the basement of the Baptist church on Almond Street. At thirteen he enrolled in a paid tuition day school in Brooklyn, Illinois, and at fourteen enrolled in the preparatory school at Oberlin College, Ohio.[11]

During the Civil War, Turner, serving as a Union officer, was wounded at the Battle of Shiloh, causing him to limp for the rest of his life. After the war, in 1866, he was asked to teach in Missouri's first tax-supported school for African Americans. Soon, he was able to found Lincoln Institute, later Lincoln University, with five thousand dollars he raised from Black veterans. The state of Missouri appointed him the state superintendent of public schools for children of color.

Turner lectured for the Equal Rights League, founded in 1866 with Frederick Douglass as a vice president, to advocate that suffrage be granted to Black men and all women. His campaigns on behalf of Republican candidates in 1871 gained him an appointment as ambassador to Liberia, where he served until 1878. He took a leading part in the huge exodus of 1879 when more than six thousand Black men, women, and children left the Deep South for settlements in Kansas, and St. Louis became a depot providing aid and comfort as they continued on the way. In 1886, in Oklahoma, Turner was asked to serve as attorney for African American members of the Cherokee nation. When he was able to bring their case before President Cleveland in 1889, it helped facilitate an award of seventy-five thousand dollars to the Black Cherokee, Delaware, and Shawnee who had not been treated fairly by their nations.[12]

Polly Berry and her two daughters survived terrible years before they were able to make their home in Missouri. Born free in Illinois around 1818, Polly Berry was only a child in the 1820s when she was among four free people kidnapped by a posse. The men carried her to Missouri and sold her into bondage. She married young, and in 1830 her daughter Lucy was born, followed by Nancy, another daughter. Although her family's liberty was stipulated in her master's will, her husband was sold south, and Nancy was kept as a servant.[13]

Polly took matters into her own hands. When she instructed her daughters to strike for liberty, Nancy fled to Canada and later married a prosperous farmer. Polly fled to Chicago, only to be seized by slave hunters. When they returned her to St. Louis, she claimed she had been kidnapped, sued in court for her freedom, and won her case.

Her daughter Lucy, when she was about twelve, was sent to live with another master. She became defiant and said: "You have no business to whip me, I don't belong to you." She also remembered her mother's advice: "My mother had so often told me that she was a free woman and that I would not die a slave. I always had a feeling of independence." Lucy also described facing her owner "who used shovel, tongs, and broomstick in

vain, as I disarmed her as fast as she picked up each weapon."
Upon hearing she was about to be sold, Lucy fled to her mother,
who concealed her with a friend.

In 1842, Polly Berry brought suit for Lucy's liberty. To prevent Lucy from fleeing, officials had her jailed for seventeen
months. Finally, after a noted abolitionist judge defended her
and three slaveholders testified for her, a Missouri court freed
her. Lucy, as an accomplished laundress, and Polly, as an accomplished seamstress, lived happily in St. Louis.

In 1849, Lucy married Zachariah Delany of Cincinnati, a marriage that lasted forty-two years. The couple had three girls and
a boy. In 1855 Lucy joined St. Louis's Methodist Episcopal
Church, and was elected president of the women's "colored society" and then president of the Daughters of Zion. Her mother,
Polly, spent her later years with Lucy's family.[14]

Kansas

From its inception as a territory in conflict it was called
"Bleeding Kansas." The brutal conflict that engulfed Kansas in
the 1850s should have warned citizens of the United States what
awaited them in less than a decade. By the time Kansas entered
the Union in January 1861, the eleven southern states had
begun to depart the United States to form a Confederacy devoted to upholding slavery. Kansas joined the Union with a
white population of 106,390 and 627 African Americans.

The first known enslaved person to come to Kansas was Malinda Noll, who arrived with her owner and her family in 1843.
She had married Nathaniel, a slave, in Kentucky, and they had
two children. By the time the family reached Fort Leavenworth,
her husband had been sold away, and she and the children had
been sold many times because they were "high-spirited, and
would never let a woman strike them."

The Noll family was moved around. "I was taken to Fort
Leavenworth some two or three years—it may be more—before
the Mexican war [of 1846]," and her daughter died a few years
later, she recalled. During her thirteen years at Fort Leavenworth, she and her owner agreed to a work arrangement that

would lead to freedom. In 1858 she managed to raise another $1,200 to purchase her twenty-two-year-old son.

An enslaved mother whose name is unknown had no option but to seize liberty through flight. With her two children, she escaped from Missouri to Lawrence, then to Topeka, Kansas. There a Missouri posse caught up with the three, whom they gagged and threw in a covered wagon. But Kansas was not Missouri, and when the mother tore off her gag and shouted for help, she was heard. A white abolitionist raced his horse to Lawrence and roused others from sleep. "We rode at full speed for nearly four hours," he recalled. They overtook the posse, three on horseback, one driving the wagon. There was an exchange of gunfire followed by hand-to-hand fighting before the posse men were subdued. The captured mother did her part. When the wagon driver tried to drive off she "sprang up [and] caught hold of him by the neck." The man ran off as rescuers caught up with the wagon.[15]

The bitter fights in Kansas made it unsafe for the normal business of slave trading. A young African American man remembered what happened at Iowa Point, Kansas, when people attempted to auction him off to the highest bidder. An antislavery posse galloped in, determined to end the auction. "Twenty-five or thirty men armed with clubs and riding horses hurrying down the ravine" clashed with the auction crowd, "and there was much brawling and cursings." He continued:

> There were many bloody noses, and some heads cracked by the clubs. It was a bunch of "free soilers" who were determined to break up the auction. The man leading the riderless horse rushed up to me and shouted, "The moment your feet touched Kansas soil, you were a free man," and, then, he ordered me to mount the horse and we rode at a fast gallop, leaving the two groups of men to fight it out.[16]

Richard Hinton, who rode with John Brown's posse in Kansas, saw that the territory provided new opportunities for escapees. Comparing it to the states bordering the Mississippi

River, he said, "Kansas opened a bolder way of escape from the southwest slave section." When armed clashes with slaveholders escalated, the Missouri owners moved their slaves southward rather than risk losing them to abolitionist bands. Kansas's enslaved population, which numbered five hundred at one point in the 1850s, slid to fifty after a few weeks of war.[17]

The business of the Underground Railroad also increased, especially with so many skilled conductors present in Kansas. In April 1859 conductor Colonel J. Bowles described the last four years of his Lawrence station, as a place where "nearly three hundred fugitives have passed through and received assistance from the abolitionists here." The previous Christmas, Bowles pointed out, twenty-four had escaped from Missouri, and eight or ten had not been able to move on due to lack of cash. Kansas stations remained crowded enough to always be in need of funds.

In 1858 a white conductor described his eight-day trip to aid fugitives:

> My hands and feet are froze, my ears are about an
> inch thick and my cheek bones are destitute of skin,
> and what is worst I have only a few hours for rest to
> day, as I must start on the road again at night fall, to
> seek a place of safety for two of my black brethren
> that I have brought this far from the land of
> bondage.[18]

In December 1858, John Brown led a raid from Osage, Kansas, into Missouri, to rescue five people. Then his raiders "went to another plantation, where we found five more slaves, took some property and two white men [who were later released]."[19]

Enslaved people in Missouri saw the growing violence in Kansas as their opportunity and began to escape northward. James B. Abbot, a white antislavery raider, called Lawrence "the best advertised antislavery town in the world."

From the earliest days of the Civil War, Kansas opened its borders to runaways from Missouri. By February 1862, African American and white Kansans formed the Emancipation League to encourage slave flight from Missouri.

African Americans in Kansas made important educational strides during the war. In Lawrence, Black refugees of all ages attended schools taught by men and women of both races, who established schools for them. By October 1863, the Kansas State Colored Convention held its first annual meeting to promote suffrage, trial by jury, and an end to discrimination. In 1864, two thousand Black Kansans celebrated their own freedom at a West Indian Emancipation Day picnic.[20]

MISSOURI Territory 1812; State 1821

Population growth:

	1810	1820	1830	1840	1850	1860
Blacks	3,618	10,569	25,660	59,814	90,040	118,503
Whites	17,227	56,017	114,795	323,888	592,004	1,063,589

KANSAS Territory 1854; State 1861

Blacks	627
Whites	106,390

Bureau of the Census, Negro Population 1790-1915 (DC, G.P.O. 1918)

---

chapter 15

From "Alien and Stranger" to U.S. Army Officer

"We're bound for freedom's light."

The early Black pioneers who traveled westward to the Ohio and Mississippi Valleys sought a life free of iron chains. In the frontier states they still found their rights and opportunities limited by unjust laws and customs. In spite of this, many made advances denied to their sisters and brothers in the East.

Then, in the 1850s, as the nation edged toward the Civil War, the new Fugitive Slave Law threatened the liberty of every African American in the United States. Further heightening racial tensions, some western states increased restrictions on Black people and made it harder for them to enter.

For the first time many eastern and western Black families talked about leaving the country, and several thousand crossed the border into Canada. In August 1854, a Black Emigration Convention drew 102 delegates to Cleveland, Ohio, for three days of meetings.

Western states were represented, and twenty-nine women were also present at this first Black convention to seriously consider the subject of leaving the United States. During its three days, delegates protested U.S. discrimination, denounced "our white American oppressors," and discussed emigration. They demanded "every political right, privilege and position" available to whites, "refused submission" to the Fugitive Slave Law, and denounced as "contemptible" the Kansas-Nebraska Act, which opened new land to slavery.[1]

Men and women representing the old Northwest Territory of the Ohio Valley, including William Lambert, played key roles in the proceedings. Its president was the Reverend William C. Monroe of Michigan, its first vice president was the Reverend William Paul Quinn of Indiana, and its second vice president was Mrs. Mary E. Bibb of Canada. With her recently deceased husband, Henry Bibb, she had settled in Canada, where they had advocated a Black exodus from the United States, and he had published a newspaper devoted to the cause.

The delegates at Cleveland also talked proudly of the identity and common heritage of people of African descent. They stated that the United States was not the land of the free and declared that their government was a slave catcher and an enemy. One speaker after another pointed out that white Americans and their elected officials had rejected the Declaration of Independence and would not voluntarily end slavery or racial discrimination.

H. Ford Douglas (or Douglass) of Illinois, twenty-four, delivered a notable speech. He took issue with leaders such as Frederick Douglass, who opposed African Americans ever leaving the United States. The young man termed himself "an unwilling exile" who wished to "seek on other shores the freedom which has been denied me in the land of my birth."

> I can hate this government without being disloyal, because it has stricken down my manhood, and treated me as a saleable commodity. I can join a foreign enemy and fight against it, without being a traitor, because it treats me as an ALIEN and a STRANGER, and I am free to avow that should such a contingency arise I should not hesitate to take any advantage in order to procure indemnity for the future.[2]

In 1858 Douglas circulated a petition in Illinois to allow Blacks to testify in courts in the state. Abraham Lincoln was one of the politicians who refused to sign the Douglas petition. During the election of 1860, the young man attacked Lincoln for being "on the side of this Slave Power" and for favoring "that infamous Fugitive Slave Law." When seven southern states seceded from the Union to form the Confederacy in February

Wilberforce College student Richard Cain and other Blacks were rejected by the U.S. Army in 1861. After the war, Cain was elected to the U.S. Congress from South Carolina.

1861, Douglas told them to "go at once" and added that there "can be no union between freedom and slavery."[3]

But less than a year later, Douglas was one of those African Americans who saw in the unfolding Civil War what President Lincoln would later call "a new birth of freedom." Long before emancipation became a Lincoln administration policy, Black men rushed to enlist. At Wilberforce College in Ohio, Richard Cain was among 115 students who tried to enlist and were told "this was a white man's war."

Later, as a member of Congress, he told fellow congressmen: "We knew that there would come a period in the history of this nation when our strong black arms would be needed."[4]

On June 19, 1862, Congress passed a law ending slavery in all federal territories in the West. One month later Congress authorized the president to "employ persons of African descent for the suppression of the rebellion." But slaves had already begun to turn the war to save the Union into a fight for freedom. Enslaved people in the southern states had fled to the Union lines seeking their own freedom and trying to turn liberty into official U.S. policy.[5]

The president's proclamation did end slavery in rebellious states and opened the U.S. armed forces to Black men. James Milton Turner, from Missouri, joined the army as one of its few Black officers and was wounded at the Battle of Shiloh. In Ohio, Sarah Jane Woodson devoted time to helping educate "contrabands," slaves who fled the southern states. In Indiana, Samuel Smothers, saying, "I feel the time has come [for] me to act rather than talk or write," joined the U.S. army.

In Michigan, as we know, George DeBaptiste recruited a regiment of Black men and spent six months training them in South Carolina. In Iowa, in 1863, Alexander Clark, whose enlistment was once rejected by Governor Samuel Kirkwood because of his color, recruited 1,153 men into the Black First Iowa Volunteer Regiment and served as their sergeant major.

In Arkansas, Black men formed a regiment that marched to this song:

> We're going out of slavery,
> We're bound for freedom's
> light.
> We mean to show Jeff Davis
> How Africans can fight.[6]

But what about H. Ford Douglas? Black volunteers were being turned down in 1861 when Douglas saw his opportunity. He had become convinced that regardless of official policy, the Union army fighting in the southern states was bound to weaken if not destroy bondage. Overcoming his alienation from his government, he decided to enlist. As a light-skinned man, he was able to join Company G of the Ninety-fifth Illinois Volunteers, a white regiment. But he found a mixed reception:

John M. Langston of Ohio (center) recruited Blacks as soldiers. At Camp Delaware in 1863 he presents "the colors" to the Fifth U.S. Colored Troops.

> . . . although I am respected by my own regiment and treated kindly by those who know me, still there are those in other regiments with whom I come in contact who have no regard for my feelings simply because I have the hated blood coursing in my veins.[7]

After emancipation, in 1863, Douglas transferred to a Black Louisiana regiment and was promoted to lieutenant and then to captain. By the end of the war Captain Douglas, in command of an African American artillery unit in Kansas, had become the state's highest-ranking Black U.S. officer.

As early as September 1861, slaves who had fled Missouri for Kansas had been greeted with open arms by U.S. senator Jim Lane, a Union commander and recruiter. Within a year Lane had formed the First Kansas Colored Infantry at Fort Lincoln.

He began to lead his new recruits in "Jayhawking" forays into
Missouri to liberate hundreds of enslaved people. By February
1863, runaways were walking across the frozen Missouri into
Kansas, and many were signing up for the U.S. Army to complete the work of emancipation. By June, the Second Kansas
Colored Infantry Regiment had been formed, and by that October one-sixth of the Black people in Kansas had been recruited into the U.S. Army.[8]

Most of the former slave recruits were volunteers. But
Captain Douglas discovered in
June 1865 that recruiters had
used force to take three-fourths
of the men in his command
from their families, starved
them until they were near ex-
haustion, and then coerced
them into joining the army. The
young officer complained to the
War Department that such
"cruel and shameless conscrip-
tion" was "in opposition to all civil and military law." He requested an immediate investigation and the discharge of his
men. Within a month the War Department completed its inves-

Some recruiters forced Black men into the U.S. Army in South Carolina (shown here) and Kansas.

tigation and mustered his men out of service.[9]

H. Ford Douglas, a son of the Ohio and Mississippi Valleys, had devoted his life to fighting injustice. To end human bondage, he was both prepared to denounce his government and ready to join its armed forces. His career began during a bleak era when his government was an enemy and a slave catcher, and denied him his rights. But he saw the dawn of a new era that allowed a Black officer to bring his protests to the War Department and gain justice for his people.

In the Battle of Fort Wagner in 1863 Black troops proved their courage to friend and foe.

ENDNOTES

Introduction

1. Gilbert Imlay, "The Adventures of Daniel Boone," in *A Topographical Description of the Western Territory of North America* (London: 1797) 34; cited in Paul M. Angle, *The New Nation Grows* (New York: Premier Books, 1960) II, 44.

2. R. Douglas Hurt, *The Ohio Frontier* (Bloomington: Indiana University Press, 1996) 55.

3. Levi Coffin, *Reminiscences of Levi Coffin* (Cincinnati: Robert Blake, 1876) 81, 92, 94.

4. Stuart Seely Sprague, ed., *The Autobiography of John P. Parker* (New York: Norton, 1996) 31.

5. Sprague.

6. Sprague.

7. Sprague, 128, 137.

8. Lewis and Milton Clarke, *Narratives of the Sufferings of Lewis and Milton Clarke* (Boston: Bela Marsh, 1846) 63.

9. Lewis and Milton Clarke, 57.

10. *Barkshire v. the state, 7 Indiana*, 389-391, cited in William Loren Katz, *The Black West* (New York: Touchstone, 1996) 35-36.

11. Katz, 57.

12. May papers, Boston Public Library, cited in Larry Garra, *The Liberty Line* (New York: University of Kentucky, 1967) 113.

Chapter 1

1. Mrs. [Juliette Magill] Kinzie, *Wau-bun: The "Early Day" in the NorthWest* (Chicago: 1856) 219-220.

2. Sidney Kaplan and Emma Nogrady Kaplan, *The Black Presence in the Era of the American Revolution* (Amherst: University of Massachusetts Press, 1989. Revised Edition) 164-165. This is the most well-researched source on the DuSable family. See also Rayford W. Logan and Michael R. Winston, eds., *Dictionary of American Negro Biography* (New York: Norton, 1982) which includes a useful bibliography.

3. Kaplan and Kaplan.

4. Kaplan and Kaplan.

5. Kaplan and Kaplan.

6. Kaplan and Kaplan, 111. See also Rayford W. Logan and Michael R. Winston, eds., *Dictionary of American Negro Biography* (New York: Norton, 1982) which includes a list of Marrant's publications on p. 425.

7. Logan and Winston, 113.

8. Logan and Winston, 115.

9. Logan and Winston, 116.

Chapter 2

1. Dwight Lowell Dumond, *Anti-slavery: The Crusade for Freedom in America* (Ann Arbor: University of Michigan Press, 1961) 98; Hurt, 273.

2. Hurt, 103.

3. Carl Waldman, *Atlas of the North American Indian* (New York: Facts on File, 1985) 114.

4. Angie Debo, *A History of the Indians of the United States* (Norman: University of Oklahoma, 1984) 89.

5. Hurt, 101-105.

6. *American State Papers, Indian Affairs* (Washington, 1832-1834) Vol. I, 1837-1838; "Military Journal of Major Ebenezer Denny," *Memoires of the Historical Society of Pennsylvania*, VII, (Philadelphia, 1860) 370-372.

7. Hurt, 103.

8. Debo, 91; Hurt, 122.

9. Debo, 92; Hurt, 139.

10. Hurt, 274-275.

11. Hurt, 276, 277.

12. Emma Lou Thornbrough, *The Negro in Indiana* (Bloomington: Indiana Historical Bureau, 1957) 6-7. This careful study finds that St. Clair's "interpretation of the Ordinance appears to be a distortion of the obvious meaning, but at the time no one successfully challenged it."

13. Thornbrough, 6-7.

14. Hurt, 281.

15. Helen M. Thurston, "The 1802 Constitutional Convention and the Status of the Negro," *Ohio History*, V. 81, #1, 15-37; Hurt 282.

16. Eugene M. Berwanger, *The Frontier Against Slavery* (Urbana: University of Illinois Press, 1967) 22.

17. Lenwood G. Davis, "Nineteenth Century Blacks in Ohio: An Historical View," *Blacks in Ohio History*, Rubin F. Westin, ed. (Columbus, Ohio: Ohio Historical Society, 1976) 5.

18. Davis, 5.

19. Berwanger, 23.

Chapter 3

1. Henry Burke, E-mail, 9/24/97.

2. E-mail research by Wilbur Norman of Zanesville, Ohio, forwarded by Henry R. Burke, 1/7/96.

3. Burke, E-mail, 1/7/97.

4. Burke, E-mail, 9/24/97.

5. David A. Gerber, *Black Ohio and the Color Line 1860-1915* (Urbana: University of Illinois Press, 1976) 10.

6. Gerber, 18.

7. Burke, E-mail, 9/24/97.

8. *Autobiography of James B. Finley; or Pioneer Life in the West*, W. P. Strickland, ed. (Cincinnati: 1854) 110-111.

9. Finley, 111.

10. Burke, E-mail, 9/24/97.

11. Donald J. Ratcliffe, "Capt. James Riley and Anti-slavery Sentiment in Ohio, 1819-1824," *Ohio History*, V. 81, #2, 276-294.

12. Ratcliffe, 280.

13. *Journal of Negro History*, Vol. V, #4 (October 1920) 485.

14. Georgiana Whyte, *Journal of Negro History*, Vol. V, #4 (October 1920) 484-485.

15. William H. Pease and Jane H. Pease, *Black Utopia: Negro Communal Experiments in America* (Madison: State Historical Society of Wisconsin, 1963) 26.

16. John L. Myers, "American Antislavery Society Agents and the Free Negro, 1833-1838," *Journal of Negro History*, Vol. LII, #3 (July 1967) 200-219.

17. Myers, 213-214; WPA Project, *The Negro in Virginia* (New York: Hastings House, 1940) 116.

18. *The North Star,* August 11, 1848.

Chapter 4

1. Arthur A. Schomburg, "Two Negro Missionaries to the American Indians," *Journal of Negro History*, Vol. XXI, #3 (October 1936) 323-326 *passim.*

2. George Cantor, "Touring the Black Past," *American Legacy* (February-March 1995) 31.

3. Bevery Gray, E-mail, 10/28/97.

4. Dumond, 158, 91.

5. Ellen N. Lawson, "Sarah Woodson Early: 19th Century Black Nationalist 'Sister,'" *UMOJA*, V. 2 (Summer 1981) in Darlene Clark Hine, Vol. III, *Black Women in United States History, III* (Brooklyn: Carlson, 1990) 815-816.

6. Ellen N. Lawson and Marlene Merrill, "Antebellum Black Coeds at Oberlin College," *Oberlin Alumni Magazine* (January-February 1980) 18-21; reprinted in Hine, 827-830.

7. Bevery Gray, E-mail, 10/28/97; Burke, phone call, 1/20/97.

8. Lawson, Oberlin, 17.

9. Lawson, 18.

10. Lawson.

11. Lawson, 19.

12. Lawson, 18-21.

13. Jesse Carney Smith, ed., *Notable Black American Women* (Detroit: Gale Research, 1992) 826-827.

14. Lawson, Oberlin, 19.

15. Lawson, 20.

16. Lawson, 21.

17. Lawson, 21-23

18. Lawson, 24-25. Also see Sarah Woodson in Hine, II, 885; Ellen N. Lawson, *The Three Sarahs: Documents of Antebellum Black College Women, 1984*; see also Woodson in Darlene Clark Hine, *Black Women in the Middle West: The Michigan Experience*, 1990.

19. Lawson, 25.

Chapter 5

1. Richard C. Wade, "Cincinnati Negroes," *Journal of Negro History*, Vol. XXXIX, #1 (1954) 43-57.

2. Carter G. Woodson, "The Negroes of Cincinnati Prior to the Civil War," *Journal of Negro History*, Vol. I (January 1916) 1-22.

3. Wade, 47-48.

4. Coffin, 522-525.

5. Woodson, 21-22.

6. Martin R. Delany, *The Condition, Elevation, Emigration and Destiny of the Colored People of the United States* (Philadelphia: 1852) 97-99.

7. Gerber, 21-22.

8. *The North Star*, August 11, 1848.

9. Coffin, 197-198.

10. Coffin, 562.

11. Coffin, 564; Herbert Aptheker, *Abolitionism: A Revolutionary Movement* (Boston: Twayne Publishers, 1989) 122.

12. Gara, 137.

13. Lawrence Grossman, "In His Veins Coursed No Bootlicking Blood: The Career of Peter H. Clark," *Ohio History*, V. 86, #2. 81.

14. Grossman, 82.

15. I. Garland Penn, *The Afro-American Press and Its Editors* (Springfield: Wiley, 1891) 78.

16. Peter Clark, *The Black Brigade of Cincinnati* (Cincinnati: Joseph P. Boyd, 1864) 4.

17. Clark, 3; see also Charles L. Blockson, *Hippocrene Guide to the Underground Railroad* (New York: Hippocrene Books, 1994).

18. James M. McPherson, *The Negro's Civil War* (New York: Pantheon, 1965) 288.

19. McPherson, 289.

20. Philip Foner, ed., *The Voice of Black America* (New York: Simon & Schuster, 1972) 451-457.

Chapter 6

1. Rev. William M. Mitchell, *The Underground Railroad* (London: 1860) 20.

2. Mitchell, 98, 146.

3. Mitchell, 39-40.

4. Mitchell 41-42.

5. Mitchell, 44-45.

6. Mitchell, 28.

7. Sprague, *passim.*

8. Dumond, 93.

9. Dumond, 91.

10. Sprague, 86.

11. Dumond, 91; Blockson, 258-259.

12. Sprague, 85.

13. Sprague, 86.

14. Sprague, 138.

15. Sprague, 9.

16. Hurt, XIV.

17. *Western Anti-Slavery Society Minute Book*, August 17, 1848, in Library of Congress, cited in Garra, 118.

18. Lewis and Milton Clarke, 34-35, 36; Janice M. Kimmel, "Break Your Chains and Fly to Freedom," *Michigan History* (January-February 1996) 22.

19. *Narrative of Henry Bibb* (New York: 1849).

20. Kimmel, 26.

21. Benjamin Quarles, *Black Abolitionists* (New York: Oxford University Press, 1969) 62.

22. *Voice of the Fugitive*; microfilm in the author's possession.

23. *Voice of the Fugitive*; *passim.*

Chapter 7

1. Dwight W. Hoover, *A Teacher's Guide to American Urban History* (Chicago: Quadrangle, 1971) 114; Blockson, 253.

2. John Malvin, *Autobiography of John Malvin* (Cleveland: Leader Printing Company, 1879), edited with an Introduction by Allan Peskin (Cleveland: Press of Western Reserve University, 1966) 4, 9.

3. Malvin, 41 footnote.

4. Malvin, 45-46.

5. Malvin, 49-50.

6. Malvin, 57.

7. Malvin, 17.

8. Malvin, 19.

9. Malvin, 65-66.

10. Aptheker, 286-288.

11. Malvin, 11.

12. Malvin, 14.

13. Theodore Clarke Smith, *The Liberty and Soil Parties in the Northwest* (New York: Longman's Green, 1997) 13, 16.

14. Aptheker, 262

15. *William Lloyd Garrison, 1805-1879, The Story of His Life Told by His Children* (New York: Century Co., 1889) III, 194-195, 200-201, 203-205.

16. Malvin, 67.

17. Malvin, 73-78.

18. Malvin, 17.

19. William J. Simmons, *Men of Mark* (Cleveland: M. Rewell, 1887) 978-979.

20. Simmons, 979-980; see also Amistead S. Pride and Clint Wilson, *A History of the Black Press* (Washington, D.C.: Howard University Press, 1996).

21. Penn, 74-75.

22. Simmons, 981-982.

23. Malvin, 13-14.

24. Malvin, 15.

25. *Journal of Negro History*, Vol. XXIII, #3 (October 1938) 428-434.

26. Malvin, 22.

Chapter 8

1. Robert M. Taylor, Jr. and Connie A. McBirney, *Peopling Indiana: The Ethnic Experience* (Indianapolis: Indiana Historical Society, 1996); "African Americans" by Emma Lou Thornbrough, 12-37.

2. Berwanger, 9.

3. Taylor and McBirney, 12.

4. Dumond, 99; Thornbrough, *The Negro in Indiana*, 8, 11.

5. Thornbrough, 1, 13-15, 17, 18.

6. Taylor and McBirney, 26, 29-30.

7. Berwanger, 20.

8. *African Repository and Colonial Journal* (Washington, D.C.) Vol. I, 127.

9. "Memoirs of William Forster" in Harlow Lindley, ed., *Indiana as Seen by Early Travellers* (Indiana Historical Collections, Vol. 3 (Indianapolis: 1916) 257-258, in Thornbrough, 100.

10. Thornbrough, 18.

11. Taylor and McBirney, 134; William Trail, "The Story of a Slave in Indiana," *The Indianian,* #3, (1899) 257-262.

12. Thornbrough, 50, 134-135, 172; Taylor and McBirney, 14.

13. Thornbrough, 35-36, 133, 136, 137, 139, 140-141, 141.

14. Thornbrough, 94, 120-121; Taylor and McBirney, 12-13.

15. Thornbrough, 70, 139; Berwanger, 45.

16. Benjamin Drew, *A North-Side View of Slavery* (Boston: J. P. Jewett, 1856) in Dorothy Sterling, ed., *Speak Out in Thunder Tones* (New York: Doubleday, 1973) 117.

17. Thornbrough, 145; Wilbur Siebert, *The Underground Railroad from Slavery to Freedom* (New York: Macmillan, 1898) 138.

18. Coffin, 111-112.

19. Coffin, 42-43; Quarles, 162-163.

20. Indianapolis *Indiana Star Sentinel*, January 4, 1851, cited in Thornbrough, 111.

21. Thornbrough, 113, 114; Frederick Douglass, *Life and Times of Frederick Douglass* (New York: Collier Books, 1962, from 1892, Third Edition) 231.

22. Thornbrough, 171-172; Blockson, 223.

23. Thornbrough, 162-164, 173-174.

24. Thornbrough, 165-166, 168, 169; Taylor and McBirney, 14; New Castle, *Courier*, August 2, 1866.

Chapter 9

1. Theodore Calvin Pease, *The Story of Illinois* (Chicago: University of Chicago, 1965) 12; John W. Allen, "Slavery and Negro Servitude in Pope County, Illinois," *Journal of the Illinois Historical Society*, Vol. 42, #4 (December 1949) 411-423.

2. Dumond, 92; Berwanger, 8, 18.

3. Richard J. Jensen, *Illinois: A Bicentennial History* (New York: Norton, 1978) 29; Allen, 414.

4. Hine, *Black Women in America*, II, 884.

5. *African Repository and Colonial Journal* (Washington, D.C.) Vol. I, 124.

6. W. Sherman Savage, "The Contest Over Slavery Between Illinois and Missouri," *Journal of Negro History*, Vol. XXVIII, #3, 7-43 and 311-325.

7. Savage, 321-325.

8. Blockson, Hippocrene, 217, 220-221; Siebert, 42.

9. Gara, 116-117, citing James H. Collins, Wilbur Siebert Papers.

10. Dumond, 225-226, 229, 232.

11. *The Legion of Liberty and Force of Truth* (New York: American Antislavery Society, 1843) 9; J. C. Power, *Early Settlers of Sangamon County* (Springfield: 1876) 303; *Sagamon Journal*, May 10, 1832.

12. John E. Washington, *They Knew Lincoln* (New York: 1942) 189-190, 202; Blockson, 224.

13. Jeff Lyon, "Generations," *Chicago Tribune Magazine* (February 23, 1992) 16; Blockson, 227.

14. Rufus Blanchard, *Discovery and Conquests of the Northwest with the History of Chicago* (Chicago: 1898) II, 207-302; Frederick Douglass's Paper, September 15, 1854.

15. Moses Dickson, *Manual of the International Order of Twelve* (St. Louis: 1891) 7-15.

16. Sterling, 147-148; Blanchard, 207-302 *passim*.

17. McPherson, 253-254; *Chicago Tribune* (May 22, 1879) 7.

Chapter 10

1. Council on Interracial Books for Children, *Chronicles of American Indian Protest* (Greenwich: Fawcett, 1971) 40-41; William Loren Katz, *Black Indians: A Hidden Heritage* (New York: Atheneum, 1986) 111.

2. Darlene Clark Hine, et al., eds., *Black Women in America* (Brooklyn: Carolson, 1993) Vol. I, 445.

3. Janice M. Kimmel, "Break Your Chains and Fly to Freedom," *Michigan History* (January-February 1996) 26.

4. Anna-Lisa Cox, "A Pocket of Freedom: Blacks in Couvert, Michigan in the Nineteenth Century," *Michigan History* (January-February 1996) 3, 17-18.

5. David M. Katzman, *Before the Ghetto* (Urbana: University of Illinois, 1973) 9-11.

6. Laura S. Haviland, *A Woman's Life-work* (Chicago: Publishing Association of Friends, 1882) 92, 116, 121, 125; Dumond, 279. In 1997 Detroit opened the largest Museum of African American History in the United States and exhibits featured its Underground Railroad stations and antislavery workers. See Robyn Meredith, "In Detroit, Black Pride Where Slaves Once Hid," *The New York Times* (Sunday, July 6, 1997) Travel Section, 8.

7. Martin R. Delany in *The North Star* (July 28, 1848), *Detroit Daily Post* (February 7, 1870); George N. Fuller, ed., *Michigan: A Centennial History of the State and Its People I* (Chicago: 1939) 360; both cited in Sylvia G. L. Dannett, *Profiles of Negro Womanhood* (New York: Educational

Heritage, Inc., 1964) I, 62-63.

8. Coffin, 366, 369, 371-372.

9. The basic information about Lambert and DeBaptiste can be found in Katherine DuPre Lump-kin, "'The General Plan Was Freedom': A Negro Secret Order on the Underground Railroad" *Phylon*, XXVIII (Spring 1967) 63-77. This study largely relies on a newspaper interview with De-Baptiste in the *Detroit Post*, May 15, 1870, and another with Lambert in the *Detroit Tribune*, January 17, 1886.

10. Herbert Aptheker, ed., *A Documentary History of the Negro People in the United States* (New York: Citadel Press, 1951) Vol. I, 233-234.

11. Thornbrough, 60, citing *DeBaptiste v. the State,* 1839; see also Logan and Winston entry for DeBaptiste.

12. DuPre Lumpkin, 70-77.

13. Lumpkin.

14. Lumpkin.

15. Berwanger, 38.

16. Aptheker, I, 460.

Chapter 11

1. Ray A. Billington, *Westward Expansion: A History of the American Frontier* (New York: Macmillan, 1967) 476-477.

2. Robert R. Dykstra, *Bright Radical Star: Black Freedom and White Supremacy on the Hawkeye Frontier* (Cambridge: Harvard University Press, 1993) 7.

3. James L. Hill, "Migration of Blacks to Iowa, 1820-1860," *Journal of Negro History*, Vol. LVI, #4 (Winter 1981-1982) 27.

4. Hill, 28.

5. Dykstra, 8.

6. Berwanger, 33.

7. Dykstra, 9; *The Legion of Liberty and Force of Truth* (New York: Antislavery Society, 1843) 9.

8. Dykstra, 13-16; Blockson, 238.

9. Dykstra, 20-21.

10. *Annals of Iowa* (April 1946) interview by Ora Williams cited in Charles L. Blockson, *The Underground Railroad* (New York: Prentice Hall, 1978) 187-188.

11. Blockson, 190-193, 239.

12. Dykstra, 18, 150-151, 173.

13. Dykstra, 197; Hill, 25.

14. Dykstra, 197-198, 224, 229.

15. Dykstra, 231, 239.

Chapter 12

1. Blockson, *Hippocrene Guide*, 270-271.

2. Gara, 120.

3. Siebert, 327-328.

4. Gara, 135-136.

5. Berwanger, 36.

6. *Heritage Wisconsin*, Wisconsin Bureau of Tourism, 1998, 24-25.

7. *Heritage Wisconsin*, 28-29.

8. *Heritage Wisconsin*, 11.

9. *Heritage Wisconsin*, 14-15.

10. Hoover, 298, 300.

Chapter 13

1. *Gopher History*, Winter, 1968-1969, "Black Men in the Fur Trade with the Indians,"1.

2. *Gopher History*, 2-4.

3. *Gopher History*, 4; Hine, et al., II, 1250.

4. *Gopher History*, 5-6.

5. William Loren Katz, *Black Women of the Old West* (New York: Atheneum, 1996) 9.

6. *Gopher History*, 6.

7. *Gopher History*, 6-8.

8. Emily O. Goodridge Grey, "The Black Community in Territorial St. Anthony: A Memoir by

Emily O. Goodridge Grey," edited by Patricia C. Harpole, *Minnesota History* (Summer 1984) Vol. 49, #2, 42-53, 46.

9. Grey, 48, 50.

10. Grey, 53

11. Grey, 50, 53.

12. *Gopher History*, 6-7.

13. William Loren Katz, *Black People Who Made the Old West* (Laurenceville, N.J.: Africa World Press, 1994) 78.

Chapter 14

1. Wade, 5.

2. Stephen E. Ambrose, *Undaunted Courage* (New York: Simon & Schuster, 1996) 118, 131, 133, 180, 198, 235, 276, 278, 309.

3. Wade, 125-127.

4. Wade, 221.

5. H. C. Bruce, *The New Man* (York, Pa.: 1895) 76.

6. Bruce, 108-109, 112.

7. Bruce, 119-120, 177.

8. Lorenzo J. Greene, Gary R. Kremer, Antonio F. Holland, *Missouri's Black Heritage* (Columbia, Mo.: University of Missouri Press, 1993. Revised Edition) 67.

9. Greene, et al., 67-68.

10. Greene, et al., 72.

11. Logan and Winston, 611; see also Gary R. Kremer, *James Milton Turner and the Promise of America* (Columbia: University of Missouri Press, 1991).

12. Logan and Winston, 72.

13. Jesse Carney Smith, 262.

14. Jesse Carney Smith, 262-263.

15. James Redpath, *The Roving Editor* (New York: Negro Universities Press, 1968, reprint of 1859 book) 314-316, 320-322, 345.

16. Uncle Mose, quoted in the *Negro History Bulletin* (March 1955) cited in Katz, *The Black West*, 108.

17. Richard J. Hinton, *John Brown and His Men* (New York: Funk & Wagnalls, 1894) 106, 172-173, 221.

18. Gara, 125.

19. John Brown, Letter, January 1859, cited in Siebert, 162.

20. Richard B. Sheridan, "From Slavery in Missouri to Freedom in Kansas," *Kansas History*, Vol. 12, #1 (Spring 1989) 28-47.

Chapter 15

1. Vincent Harding, *There Is a River* (New York: Harcourt Brace, 1981) 185-189. See also John H. Bracey, Jr., August Meier, and Elliott Rudwick, eds., *Black Nationalism in America* (New York: Bobbs-Merrill) 87-110. These two sources carefully document this convention's proceedings.

2. Harding, 187-189.

3. McPherson, 5-7.

4. *Congressional Record*, 43rd Congress, First Session, cited in Katz, *The Black West*, 112-113.

5. Sheridan, 28-47.

6. Charles H. Wesley and Patricia W. Romero, *Negro Americans in the Civil War* (New York: Publishers Company, Inc, 1967) 162-163.

7. McPherson, 11-12.

8. Sheridan, 43-47.

9. Quintard Taylor, *In Search of the Racial Frontier* (New York: Norton, 1988) 100.

BIBLIOGRAPY

Allen, John W. "Slavery and Negro Servitude in Pope County, Illinois." *Journal of the Illinois Historical Society* 42, no. 4 (December 1949).

Ambrose, Stephen A. *Undaunted Courage: Merriwether Lewis, Thomas Jefferson and the Opening of the American West*. New York: Simon & Schuster, 1996.

Aptheker, Herbert. *Abolitionism: A Revolutionary Movement*. Boston: Twayne Publishers, 1989.

Aptheker, Herbert, ed. *A Documentary History of the Negro People in the United States*. New York: Citadel Press, 1951.

Berwanger, Eugene H. *The Frontier Against Slavery*. Urbana: University of Illinois Press, 1967.

Bibb, Henry. *Narrative of Henry Bibb*. New York: 1849.

Billington, Ray A. *Westward Expansion: A History of the American Frontier*. New York: Macmillan, 1967.

"Black Men in the Fur Trade with the Indians," *Gopher History* (Winter 1968-1969).

Blanchard, Rufus. *Discovery and Conquests of the Northwest with the History of Chicago*. Chicago: 1898.

Blockson, Charles L. *Hippocrene Guide to the Underground Railroad*. New York: Hippocrene Books, 1994.

Blockson, Charles L. *The Underground Railroad*. New York: Prentice Hall, 1987.

Bontemps, Arna, and Jack Conroy. *Anyplace But Here*. New York: Hill and Wang, 1966.

Bracey, John H., Jr., August Meier, and Elliott Rudwick, eds. *Black Nationalism in America*. New York: Bobbs-Merrill, 1970.

Bruce, H. C., *The New Man*. York, Pa.: 1895.

Carroll, Joseph C. "William Trail: An Indiana Pioneer." *Journal of Negro History,* Vol. XXIII (October 1938).

Cheek, William. "John Mercer Langston: Black Protest Leader and Abolitionist." *Civil War History* XVI (March 1970).

Clarke, Lewis, and Milton Clarke. *Narratives of the Sufferings of Lewis and Milton Clarke*. Boston: Bela Marsh, 1846.

Clark, Peter. *The Black Brigade of Cincinnati*. Cincinnati: Joseph P. Boyd, 1864.

Coffin, Levi. *Reminiscences of Levi Coffin*. Cincinnati: Robert Clarke, 1876.

Council on Interracial Books for Children. *Chronicles of American Indian Protest*. Greenwich: Fawcett, 1971. 40-41.

Cox, Anna-Lise. "A Pocket of Freedom: Blacks in Couvert, Michigan in the Nineteenth Century." *Michigan History* (January-February 1996).

Davidson, John Nelson. *Negro Slavery and the Underground Railroad in Wisconsin*. Milwaukee: Parkman Club, 1891.

Davis, Harry E. "John Malvin, A Western Reserve Pioneer." *Journal of Negro History*, Vol. XXIII (October 1938).

Davis, Lenwood G. "Nineteenth Century Blacks in Ohio: An Historical View." In Rubin F. Westin, ed. *Blacks in Ohio History*. Columbus: Ohio Historical Society, 1976.

Debo, Angie. *A History of the Indians of the United States*. Norman: University of Oklahoma Press, 1984.

Delany, Martin R. *The Condition, Elevation, Emigration and Destiny of the Colored People of the United States*. Philadelphia: published by the author, 1852.

Douglass, Frederick. *Life and Times of Frederick Douglass*. New York: Collier Books, 1962.

Drew, Benjamin. *A North-Side View of Slavery*. Boston: J. P. Jewett, 1856.

Dumond, Dwight Lowell. *Antislavery: The Crusade for Freedom in America*. Ann Arbor: University of Michigan Press, 1961.

DuPre Lumpkin, Katherine. "'The General Plan was Freedom': A Negro Secret Order on the Underground Railroad." *Phylon* XXVIII (Spring 1967).

Dykstra, Robert R. *Bright Radical Star: Black Freedom and White Supremacy on the Hawkeye Frontier.* Cambridge: Harvard University Press, 1993.

Foner, Philip, ed. *The Voice of Black America.* New York: Simon & Schuster, 1972.

Franklin, John Hope. *From Slavery to Freedom.* New York: Knopf, 1980.

Gara, Larry. *The Liberty Line.* Lexington: University of Kentucky, 1967.

Garrison, William Lloyd. *William Lloyd Garrison, 1805-1879, The Story of His Life Told by His Children.* New York: Century Co., 1889.

Gerber, David A. *Black Ohio and the Color Line 1860-1915.* Chicago: University of Illinois Press, 1976.

Greene, Lorenzo J., Gary R. Kremer, Antonio F. Holland. *Missouri's Black Heritage.* Columbia: University of Missouri Press, 1993. Revised Edition.

Grossman, Lawrence. "'In His Veins Coursed No Bootlicking Blood': The Career of Peter H. Clark." *Ohio History* 86, no. 2.

Harpole, Patricia, C., ed. "The Black Community in Territorial St. Anthony: A Memoir by Emily O. Goodridge Grey." *Minnesota History* 49, no. 2 (Summer 1984).

Harding, Vincent. *There Is a River.* New York: Vintage Books, 1981.

Haviland, Laura S. *A Woman's Life-work.* Chicago: Publishing Assocation of Friends, 1882.

Heritage Wisconsin, Wisconsin Bureau of Tourism, 1998.

Hill, James L. "Migration of Blacks to Iowa, 1820-1860." *Journal of Negro History*, Vol. LVI, #4 (Winter 1981-82).

Hine, Darlene Clark, et al., eds. *Black Women in America: An Historical Encyclopedia.* Brooklyn: Carlson, 1992.

Hine, Darlene Clark, and Kathleen Thompson. *A Shining Thread of Hope.* New York: Broadway Books, 1998.

Hinton, Richard J. *John Brown and His Men.* New York: Funk & Wagnalls, 1894.

Hoover, Dwight W. *A Teacher's Guide to American Urban History.* Chicago: Quadrangle, 1971.

Hurt, R. Douglas. *The Ohio Frontier.* Bloomington: Indiana University Press, 1996.

Kaplan, Sidney, and Emma Nogrady Kaplan. *The Black Presence in the Era of the American Revolution.* Amherst: University of Massachusetts Press, 1989. Revised Edition.

Katz, William Loren. *Black Indians: A Hidden Heritage.* New York: Atheneum, 1986.

Katz, William Loren. *Black People Who Made the Old West.* Laurenceville, NJ: Africa World Press, 1994.

Katz, William Loren. *The Black West.* New York: Touchstone, 1996.

Katz, William Loren. *Black Women of the Old West.* New York: Atheneum, 1995.

Katzman, David M. *Before the Ghetto.* Urbana: University of Ilinois, 1973.

Kaufman, Kenneth C. *Dred Scott's Advocate: A Biography of Roswell M. Field.* Columbia: University of Missouri Press, 1996.

Kimmel, Janice M. "Break Your Chains and Fly to Freedom." *Michigan History* (January-February 1996).

Kinzie, Mrs. John [Juliette Magill]. *Wau-bun: The "Early Day" in the NorthWest.* Chicago: 1856.

Kremer, Gary R. *James Milton Turner and the Promise of America.* Columbia: University of Missouri Press, 1991.

Langston, John Mercer. *From the Virginia Plantation to the National Capitol.* Hartford: American Publishing Company, 1894.

Lawson, Ellen N. "Sarah Woodson Early: 19th Century Black Nationalist 'Sister.'" *UMOJA* 2 (Summer 1981).

Lawson, Ellen N., and Marlene Merrill. "Antebellum Black Coeds at Oberlin College." *Oberlin Alumni Magazine* (January-February 1980).

Lindley, Harlow, ed. *Indiana as Seen by Early Travellers.* Indianapolis: Indiana Historical Collections 3, 1916.

Logan, Rayford W., and Michael R. Winston, eds. *Dictionary of American Negro Biography.* New York: Norton, 1982.

Malvin, John. *Autobiography of John Malvin.* Cleveland: Leader Printing Company, 1879. Reprint edition with an introduction by Allan Peskin. Cleveland: Press of Western Reserve University, 1966.

McPherson, James M. *The Negro's Civil War*. New York: Pantheon, 1965.

Mitchell, Rev. William M. *The Underground Railroad*. London: W. Tweedie, 1860.

Myers, John L. "American Antislavery Society Agents and the Free Negro, 1833-1838." *Journal of Negro History,* Vol. LII, #3 (July 1967).

Pease, Theodore Calvin. *The Story of Illinois*. Chicago: University of Chicago, 1965.

Pease, William H., and Jane H. Pease. *Black Utopia: Negro Communal Experiments in America*. Madison: State Historical Society of Wisconsin, 1963.

Penn, I. Garland. *The Afro-American Press and Its Editors*. Springfield: Wiley, 1891.

Porter, Kenneth Wiggins. *The Negro on the American Frontier*. New York: Arno Press, 1971.

Pride, Amistead S., and Clint Wilson. *A History of the Black Press*. Washington, D.C.: Howard University Press, 1996.

Quarles, Benjamin. *Black Abolitionists*. New York: Oxford University Press, 1969.

Ratcliffe, Donald J. "Capt. James Riley and Anti-slavery Sentiment in Ohio, 1819-1824." *Ohio History* 81, no. 2.

Redpath, James. *The Roving Editor*. New York: Negro Universities Press, 1968. Reprint of 1859 book.

Savage, W. Sherman. "The Contest Over Slavery Between Illinois and Missouri." *Journal of Negro History,* Vol. XXVIII, #3.

Schomburg, Arthur A. "Two Negro Missionaries to the American Indians." *Journal of Negro History*, Vol. XXI (October 1936).

Sheridan, Richard B. "From Slavery in Missouri to Freedom in Kansas." *Kansas History* 12, no. 1 (Spring 1989).

Siebert, Wilbur Henry. *The Mysteries of Ohio's Underground Railroad*. Columbus: Long's College Book Company, 1951.

Siebert, Wilbur Henry. *The Underground Railroad from Slavery to Freedom*. New York: Macmillan, 1898.

Simmons, William J. *Men of Mark*. Cleveland: M. Rewell, 1887.

Smith, Jesse Carney, ed. *Notable Black American Women*. Detroit: Gale Research, 1992.

Smith, Theodore Clarke. *The Liberty and Soil Parties in the Northwest*. New York: Longman's Green, 1897.

Sprague, Stuart Seely, ed. *His Promised Land: The Autobiography of John P. Parker, Former Slave and Conductor on the Underground Railroad*. New York: Norton, 1996.

Sterling, Dorothy, ed. *Speak Out in Thunder Tones*. New York: Doubleday, 1973.

Strickland, W. P. *Autobiography of James B. Finley; or Pioneer Life in the West*. Cincinnati: 1854.

Thornbrough, Emma Lou. "African Americans." In Robert M. Taylor, Jr. and Connie A. McBirney's *Peopling Indiana: The Ethnic Experience*. Indianapolis: Indiana Historical Society, 1996.

Thornbrough, Emma Lou. *The Negro in Indiana*. Bloomington: Indiana Historical Bureau, 1957.

Thurston, Helen M. "The 1802 Constitutional Convention and the Status of the Negro." *Ohio History* 81, no. 1.

Trail, William. "The Story of a Slave in Indiana." *The Indianian, 1899,* no. 3.

Wade, Richard C. *Slavery in the Cities*. New York: Oxford University Press, 1964.

Washington, John E. *They Knew Lincoln*. New York: 1942.

Wesley, Charles H., and Patricia W. Romero. *Negro Americans in the Civil War*. New York: Publishers Company, 1967.

Westin, Rubin F., ed. *Blacks in Ohio History*. Columbus: Ohio Historical Society, 1976.

Winks, Robin W. *The Blacks in Canada*. New Haven: Yale University Press, 1971.

Woodson, Carter G. "The Negroes of Cincinnati Prior to the Civil War." *Journal of Negro History,* Vol. I, #1.

INDEX